Lab Rat Manifesto is the culmination of a lifetime of hard living and constant dissolution. This content is not for the meek or those with pacemakers. Most of the literature contained within the pages of this novel will either make you laugh and relate, or make you throw the book down in disgust. The stories within Lab Rat Manifesto match the angst dullness and insanity that fill the lives of people shunned and living on the outskirts of society in today's America. This is just one loser's documentation of that.

This novel was written while mainly hung over on lined white paper from a cramped apartment in Myrtle Beach, South Carolina

Contents

Lab Rat Manifesto

Brett Stout

Self-Financed and Published by the Cooterific Publishing Company

Distributed by Lulu.com

Thanks Mom

Layout and Design by Brett Stout, Jezabel, and Sam Hewitt

Edited by Brett Stout and Ron Wagner

Front Photograph by Brett Stout

Send Hate Mail to dbstout@coastal.edu

Official Site: http://www.myspace.com/brettiscooterific

First Edition 2007

ISBN 978-0-6151-5279-0

Dedicated to all those who have been excluded at some point or another

You said one too many things to me tonight. There I was sitting on the couch trying to watch Sanford and Son reruns and you just wouldn't stop belittling me. The final straw was calling me a "Psychotic cocksucker." After that, I couldn't control myself. I threw your frail little body into the wall and your fragile ninety-eight pounds bounced off that and onto the dirty living room floor. I instantly got on top off you, unzipped my pants and pulled my limp cock out and smeared it on your face at first, but then I started smacking you with it. I must have done it one time too many times, because before I knew what had happened, you bit into my cock like a rabid dog. I yelled "Fuck" as loud as I could and balled up my fist and punched you in the eye. We now sit at the kitchen table staring at each other, but saying nothing. You have an old frozen T-bone steak on your face and I have a Neosporin laced gauze pad on my dick.

+++

Used condoms litter the park where I used to play as a child. Crack bags and old newspapers are on the grass and in the sewers. An early morning dew gives cover to the bums camping out in the grass. Miller and Budweiser are now our primary sponsors. Little black children swing on razor blades. STD infected cross dressers throwing a Frisbee. Spot is dead and gone so there is no one to catch it. Did it make a sound? Ghetto blasters and gold chains mend the fences. A deflated basketball sits by itself in the corner awaiting a Jesus like resurrection. The traces of hand jobs on a bench are all that's left. Abandoned buildings and cigarette wrappers are my invitation parade.

+++

Awoken like a bad dream

Wiping crust from eyes

Rising

Scratching my ball sack

Stumbling towards the door

Had you come back to me?

Could that soft knock be you?

I covered my cock with my hand just in case it wasn't

A turn of the lock and twist of the handle

Revealed

A folded up pamphlet

And not the love of my life

Fucking Jehovah's Witnesses!

Don't they have better things to do?

At nine in the morning

+++

The stove is heating up. My mid range of pain is only a matter of minutes away. I select a freshly washed small carving knife from the kitchen drawer. A man is only as good as his tools allow him to be, in my mind. I place the edge of the knife on the burner and wait. Patience is a virtue my mother always said to me as a young child. That's really one of the few things worth a shit she ever said to me. I watch patiently as the knife turns a glowing orange and I decide to pick it up. The handle of the knife burns my hand slightly but I pick it up anyway. The burning brings the pain with it. I pull down my pants and look at my cock one last time. I place my hand on the kitchen counter to balance myself and I spread my fingers out slightly. I look at the glowing knife and then I look at my cock. I start to think and I start to lose my nerve. It's now or never I tell myself.

+++

The sun never shines anymore

These days

Blackness all the time

Constant

It soon brings the boredom and feelings of

Isolation and laziness with it

I sit here

All day

Every day

Nothing to do

No one worth talking to

Just me

Here

Sitting in stained blue underwear

Finding comfort in ginger ale and cheap cigarettes

+++

Finding out that you have an STD on Christmas is a fucked up present. I used to go to bed early on Christmas Eve and wake up and find a new bike or skateboard, but now I wake up and find white shit coming out of my dick. I already disliked Christmas, but today it's the worst day of the year. Walking into my Mom's room and waking her up at seven in the morning and telling her that I might have an STD fucking sucked. Of course nothing is open today, so I guess I will have to just deal with it. I don't have insurance because I'm fucking poor, so going to the emergency room is out of the question. It feels like fucking razor blades are trying to come out of my dick every time I have to take a piss. That fucking Italian prostitute in Amsterdam was probably a mistake thinking back on it now. This might be the last straw. Maybe a little life change is in order. As always, with me it takes the absolute worst possible situation to happen for me to learn a lesson. The only thing is that I like getting drunk and fucking sluts, it's the only thing I'm any good at really. I must have been bad, Merry Christmas!

+++

Box cutters and two cigarettes left

An ink pen that doesn't write anymore

The bleeding can only come from me

Spare change and a lottery ticket

That didn't make me a millionaire

A clothespin that never held clothes

And three dollars that haven't paid for anything yet

Two pairs of scissors that may kill someone

One day but not yet

The ashtray is full and on fire

+++

My wife had a child on Monday. I wasn't there to see the spectacle of course. I was at the bar getting hammered and hitting on girls half my age. I was fucking that girl in the ass probably around the same time that he was born. I came to see it a few days after. It didn't even look like me at all. We went home that day. You said you were tired and needed to get some rest. Taking care of "It" was my duty for the next few hours. I was lounging on the couch trying to watch Married with Children reruns when "It" started crying. "It" wouldn't stop fucking crying. I turned the volume up on the TV with the remote and "It" seemed to cry even louder. I was furious and went to the kitchen to get another beer. The crying continued as I cracked the top off another PBR in the bottle. I was looking for a towel to clean up the PBR I had spilled on the floor when I spotted a shiny butcher knife in one of the kitchen drawers. I sat my beer down and grabbed the knife. I went to the small little bed "It" was crying in and told "It" to "Shut the fuck up you little bastard child." "It" started crying even louder now. I stabbed "It" right in the chest. I was amazed at how easy the knife pierced "Its" raw pink baby flesh. The crying was mixed with gurgling sounds now as blood had flowed into his lungs. My next hack was near the neck and "Its" head came rolling off his body like a miniature bowling ball. I laid the knife in the crib and went back to watching Married with Children. Damn, that Al Bundy is a funny guy!

+++

Young girls at play in an abandoned field

A child molester hides

Under a rock

Peering

Waiting like a Cobra for the right moment to strike

Pull your pants down sweetheart

This won't hurt a bit

This is bigger than your lollipop

But the taste is just as sweet

+++

While we were fucking at 7:25 this morning you asked me to smack you. I closed my fingers together and slapped the living shit out of you right between your eyebrow and your temple. You started crying and said "I didn't mean my fucking face Brett," and then you slapped me in my jaw as revenge.

+++

Playing near the swing set

The slide and kickball

Get old after doing them

Every day

Five days a week

We take a walk

In the woods near the school

We sit in dirt

I play with my G.I. Joe Snake-Eyes action figure

I throw him in a puddle and pretend that he can swim

I dry him off on my shirt

We stare at each other

We both know why we came out here

But we say nothing

You stand up

And slide down your little white panties

I lean over and look down

I see a little bit of pink skin

And some weird looking lips

I take my Snake-Eyes action figure

And move him down your panties

His black head and torso disappear

Into you

I pull him out and marvel at him

Your panties slide back up

I pull him closer and

Sniff him

It was a weird smell

I had never smelled before

I put him back in my pocket

We hold hands and walk back to the swing set

Only we know what happened

That day

Out there in the field

+++

I always knew that I was a loser, but lately I've been getting a lot of reminders about it. I got done with work the other night. Another night filled with slaving over a hot grill cooking bad food for worse people. I finished up and had a few beers afterwards at the bar next door like I usually do. There's nothing like a cold PBR when your shirt is stained with sweat and you have chicken guts all over your work shoes. I had five or six beers, just enough to get a decent little buzz on. I said goodbye to the usual group of drunks that are always in there and I headed out the door. Ever since I got that DUI a few months ago, I've been riding a shitty old ten-speed Huffy that I found at the Salvation Army thrift store for fifteen bucks. I started peddling pretty slowly down 10th Avenue and then picked up the speed a little when I turned a quick left down an alleyway. Out of nowhere, I felt a push and then I went flying off of my bike and crashed head first onto the pavement. I didn't know what the fuck had just happened. I just laid there for a few seconds trying to gather my thoughts. I lifted my head up and I saw these two teenagers standing above me laughing at me and pointing their little fingers in my direction.

"What the fuck is your problem?" I asked.

"Why did you assholes push me down?"

They didn't say anything and just kept laughing at me. I made it to my knees and started to get up to my feet. The two little assholes went running off down the alleyway. In my condition there was no way I was going to catch them.

"You fucking little punks!"

"If I ever see you little cocksuckers again I'm gonna hit you in the head with a brick."

I sat on the curb trying to get my shit together. I smoked a cigarette and felt the blood dripping onto my arm from my gashed forehead. I managed to peddle home somehow, very slowly. I didn't see the little assholes anywhere on the way home. I got home and looked in the mirror. The side of my head was all busted up and bleeding and my eye was all red. I probably had some internal bleeding behind my eye or something. But, oh well, I hate doctors and I don't have insurance anyway so fuck it. I sat on the couch with a bag of ice on my head and cold beer in my hand nursing my wounds.

"Goddamn punks!"

+++

Me and the wife were sitting in the living room eating the TV dinners she had cooked. It was the usual Hungry Man roast beef which was pretty tasty. Then there were the soggy fake mashed potatoes, bland corn, and a small square brownie for desert. The wife was flipping through channels and landed upon the cable access channel. They were flashing pictures of recent guys arrested for soliciting prostitutes in the county. I had a mouth full of a potatoes and corn when I saw my drunken mug shot flash upon the TV screen.

+++

I wake up everyday and eat the gun

Russian roulette is more fun

Played alone

And in silence

The chambers click

But the bullets are being difficult

These days

Just like the women in my life

+++

I was in this shitty store called the Dollar Tree yesterday while I waited on my chicken fried rice at the Chinese place next door. I was just wasting time but I did find a few things that I was looking for, like a scrub brush and a pack of rubber bands. As I was checking out, I noticed a rack of home pregnancy tests behind the counter. What kind of cheap piece of shit buys a pregnancy test kit at a store where everything is ninety-nine cents or less? I was very close to buying one since I thought it was so fucking insane. I might have the balls to do it the next time I'm in there waiting on my Chinese food from next door.

+++

I had to take a shit

After my swimming lesson

There was nowhere

To take a shit though

So I just shit my pants

On the side of a grassy hill

Near the pool

I sat there for three hours

Shit running down my legs

While the flies were gathering their forces

My Mom showed up drunk as usual

And yelled at me

She made me walk the two miles home

Shit fell out of my pants the whole time

And stained my shoes

My cousin laughed at me when I finally got home

I just looked at her

As I took off my clothes

I threw my shit filled underwear at her

When her back was turned

Revenge is the only road to travel sometimes

+++

You begged for it on your face. I pulled out just in time to give you what you wanted. What was it like having my cum all over you? You seemed to like it. I just sat there and watched in amazement at the spectacle. A weird smile protruded on my face. I scooped up what you couldn't get and you sucked it off my fingers. You smiled back at me.

+++

I'd just walked outside of the arts and craft store A.C. Moore on a cold Tuesday afternoon at 2 p.m. I got the value pack of cheap royal blue colored paint brushes so I could continue working on a few paintings that I was doing. I find it's easier to use cheap shitty brushes and just throw them away after I leave them out for days on end with paint on them that I'm too lazy to wash off. I don't do this on purpose, but that's the way it always ends up since I paint only in the late night hours. I had just gotten inside of my car and had turned the ignition switch and rolled down the window halfway since I had just lit a cigarette. As I went to ash for the first time, I heard a lot of commotion to the right of me. There was a large black lady carrying two large bags who seemed to be just screaming for no reason. I turned my CD player down and rolled down my window entirely so I could try and figure out what she was doing. I noticed that she was directing the yelling at some lady getting into a large white SUV parked three places to the right of me.

"Hey bitch don't you ever talk about God that way."

"You're the kinda person that ain't going to heaven."

"You ain't going to heaven, you're going hell bitch."

The lady in the white SUV said a few things back to her that I couldn't hear. But the black lady kept screaming at her even though she had rolled up her windows and was trying to pull out. The black lady walked behind my car and I heard her say once again "Bitches like that ain't getting into heaven." I never could really figure out what that was all about, but I do know this is why I avoid public places during normal business hours.

+++

Johnny grabbed several dollars and a handful of change from a cup that sits in the kitchen as he is about to walk out of the front door of his apartment.

"Johnny don't go."

"I have to baby; they've left me no choice."

"Maybe you have to be a man to understand why I have to do this."

"There's no way that fucking asshole Bill from work can eat more triple stack cheeseburger combo meals than I can."

"Get the toilet paper ready for me sweet tits."

"I'll be shitting all night after this."

"Anything for you Johnny."

"I'm headed to Wendy's; I'll be back in a flash."

"Keep that pussy warm for me while I'm away."

Johnny finally escapes his girlfriend and speeds down Highway 501 towards the nearest Wendy's.

+++

Fuck you

Yes, you

Jesus was a fag

I read that Paul gave him a blowjob

In Bethlehem

He never existed

And everything you believe in

Is a scientific farce

Faith is a waste of time

You Southern piece of redneck shit

Simple Minds

Your frontal lobe

Not the 80's band

American Idol fan?

Kill yourselves

While driving and talking about your

Sad pathetic life on a cell phone

Text is bullshit

And costs me ten cents

Stop sending them

Wal Mart is full of cheap ass losers

9/11 made me laugh

And made for great entertainment

Where's my popcorn?

Republicans are lame ignorant racists

Fuck "Dubya" and Dick Cheney

Give him some coke and

The other a shotgun loaded

Commit suicide please

Americans are the real terrorists

Fuck the troops

They deserve to die

Cunt is a great word

If used properly in a sentence

Aborted fetuses make a great art medium

Dance music sucks

And your designer mall clothes are lame

Your mother likes anal sex

Ask your dad

Kiss your mother with that mouth?

Cancer is funny

I bet someone in your family has it

New Orleans got what they deserved

Everyone hates poor niggers anyways

Dead animal carcasses are always better

Served hot

Paris Hilton and her dog

And I want to go see Maury Kenny's fat pussy

Play a great show

Can I stick this pencil in your eye?

+++

Some guy called me trying to collect a debt of two thousand dollars today. I said Brett Stout moved out months ago and hung up the phone. I'm hoping no more of those bastards have my phone number. I thought I moved around and changed my number enough for them to never find me. I guess my luck is tapped out at the moment.

+++

"Hi Susan, how's it going?"

"Oh pretty good there Brett, how are you?"

"I'm ok, minus my little problem."

"Oh yea, it's a rash, right?"

"Yea, it's a rash."

"Alrighty, just sign this and we'll get you back to see a doctor as soon as we can."

"Ok thanks."

I find a corner seat in the doctor's office and sit down. CNN Headline News is blasting from a TV above my head. I watch students come in and talk for a second at the front desk and then they sit down. None of them sit down near me though, and I suppose that's a good thing. A dumb looking guy comes in wearing a black bookbag. He talks loudly about how his girlfriend has strep throat and now he thinks he does as well. He coughs a few times loudly and then pulls out his cell phone and talks loudly to a female on the other end.

"No, I have to stay here for my appointment."

"She says I shouldn't leave."

"I don't know, I just want to come back in half an hour."

"No, just don't come."

"I'll just sit here, cough-cough."

This guy is a retard. You fucking douche bag, no you can't leave and come back in thirty minutes if you're a walk-in appointment. The nurse said it will probably be a half an hour wait, but you never know since you didn't have an appointment in the first place jerk off. Fuck, I swear there are no more inept people in the world than college kids. I slowly realize that my college degree isn't really worth a shit if morons like that graduate from them. I slowly open up my new Albert Camus book and begin on page one. I crease the book so it's easier to read. The glued pages slowly fall out of place and act as if they want to come out. By page thirty-four my eyes begin to water and my vision fails me. I needed a break from Camus for a second. CNN is talking about the Anna Nicole death and the custody battle over that fat slut's kid. I could care less at this point. Thirty-five minutes had passed and I was no further down the line to see the doctor. The coughing idiot is called next. How the fuck did he get in ahead of me? I was ahead of him by two minutes through the door. Fuck it, I would rather him go than sit here and hack and cough all over me. The last thing I need is strep throat given to me from that buffoon. I go back to Camus. The clock above the nurse's station slowly passes by. I glance up to it every five pages or so. By page sixty-eight I had been there over an hour. I watch a black girl being called back while a white girl walks in to take her place. Other people come and go but I pay no mind to it. I'm entranced in Camus. He's one of the few authors that can completely keep my attention for long periods of time, which is why I always have one of his books on me in shitty situations like this. Four pages back into Camus and I see an angel walk through the door "My god look at that fucking hot piece of ass" I think to myself. She had the most perfect body I have seen on a girl in a long time. She was gorgeous, absolutely gorgeous. She wore a white tank top and jeans. I could see her stomach where the tank top exposed her belly button, and my god it was amazing! I tried to overhear what she and her friend and the nurse were talking about but I couldn't. As it turned out, her ugly blonde haired friend was the one seeing the doctor; she was just along for the ride I suppose. They signed some papers and then made their way towards me. She sat two chairs down from me with her ugly blonde haired friend to her right. I tried to go back to Camus, but I couldn't concentrate on the words in front of me. All I could do was look at this girl and think about fucking her in every nasty perverted way possible. I wondered what her pussy tasted like and whether she liked it in the ass or not. I kept staring at her, I couldn't help it. Thank god she didn't see me. I skipped words and then sentences as I couldn't concentrate while thinking about cumming in this perfect girl's mouth. My dick slowly started moving up my lower torso. I couldn't help it, I really couldn't. By page ninety-five I had a full hard on. I tried adjusting my pants and I pulled my shirt down a little so it wasn't too obvious. The clock slowly crept by as I pretended to read Camus. The door opens and the nurse pokes her head out.

"Brett Stout the doctor will see you now."

"Fuck, just a second!"

+++

Diffusing your indifference

For the sake of future humanity

More than 2.5 kids

Continuing the same inept

Traditions formally passed

Down from previous generations

Weakness through faith

And Sunday mornings spent

Talking to Jesus

Pro life opinions

Racism

And Nascar

Are the educations

Of your more than 2.5 children

Raised in the small towns

Of the South

It's pathetic but true

The same as it was back in 1979

It never changes

Strom Thurmond might be dead

South Carolina

But his beliefs still haunt and

Radiate from the trailer parks

Of the small towns that litter

The South Carolina low country

Still voting for

Your majority elected

Republican representatives

That sends

Your poor racist

Children

To their sand brushed deaths

Eight thousand miles

Away

From the low country

Of South Carolina

+++

This girl that I had been seeing lately said that she wanted to play a game of role-play the next time we hung out. I got a call on Wednesday night from her. She said after much thinking the past week she finally came up with something that would get her off big time. She showed up at my door around 9 p.m. with a large box in her hands. I took the box from her and sat it on the kitchen table. I opened it up and pulled out what seemed to be a WWII Nazi Germany soldier's uniform. There was large dress underneath that. She said "Hey let's play Adolph and Eva, it will be a blast! The thought of dead Jews makes my pussy wet baby."

+++

Just a few more

Just a few more strokes

I almost thought I was there

Fuck!

Add more lotion

To hand

Proceed from hand

To cock

Up and down

And up and down

Come on damn it

We were almost there

So I could shoot my wad

And get on with my life

Take a shower and relax

And watch reruns of the X-Files

On TNT

Up and down

And up and down

Add more lotion to cock

From hand to cock

Up and down

And up and down

Turn the volume up

On the speakers

Where the sounds of cheap

Porno

Are coming out of

I'm almost there

Up and down

One more time

Fuck!!!!

Yes!!!!!!!

A white puddle now lies

In folded toilet paper

Where are my smokes?

+++

When I got home tonight my roommate told me that he had smoked some crack earlier in the day. I asked why he did it. He said he didn't know, but it seemed like a good idea when he was walking home drunk and a black guy offered him some. I said "That was a weird thing to do out of nowhere," as I stumbled into my room and vomited on the floor a few minutes later.

+++

I was told that I got drunk and made out with a girl that I didn't know. I was told that I pulled her hair until she screamed. I was told that I followed her into the bathroom and tried to make out with her some more in there. I was told that she was freaked out by me and left. I was told I spit on a waitress when she brought me my last beer. I was told that I spit on my bar tab when it was handed to me. I was told that I said the whole table of people I was sitting with could fuck off. I was told that my friends tried to take my keys away from me. I was told that I said I was fine and could drive home no problem, and to not worry about me since I was a great drunk driver. I was told that I went to Pizza Shack and ordered a large pepperoni pizza that I paid for with loose change. I remember getting pulled over by the cops. I remember lying quite well for a drunk. I remember the cop said my pizza smelled good. I remember the cop saying that I could go since I lived right down the street. I remember not knowing why he let me go. I remember eating pizza naked on the couch and then masturbating. I remember cumming in my hand and dropping some of it on the floor and trying to clean it up with a towel. I remember passing out on the couch watching Bill Maher on HBO. I remember why I don't drink Vodka anymore.

+++

My co-worker Marvin was bent over a manhole on Peachtree Street here in Atlanta. Me and the other guy that I worked with whose name was Johnny had been fucking with Marvin all day to pass the time. Trust me when I say that we would do anything to pass the time. That's the nature of doing really shitty construction work at seven in the morning. You find the dumbest redneck you can and fuck with his head all day and sometimes weeks or months. One time me and Johnny had this redneck electrician convinced we were gay for a month and a half. That was until my asshole boss Bill told him that we were just fucking with him. I have to admit I do a good gay lisp, but that doesn't make me gay, right? Ok, back to the original story. So Marvin was bending down looking into a city of Atlanta manhole and I snuck up behind him and put my ass in his face and made a farting sound with my mouth. Marvin had reached his end with me I guess and he got so pissed off that he called my boss Bill and told him he was sending me back to the office. Marvin said "I could take that other motherfucker Johnny with me as well." So me and Johnny went back to the office on Arizona Avenue with the big green plumbing sign in front and went into Bill's office. Bill didn't seem that pissed off at us, but scolded us a little for being fuck-ups on the job and doing stupid shit to pass the time. This was on a Thursday and Bill told both of us to take the next day off and come back in on Monday. We went down the street to one of our favorite watering holes and proceeded to get really drunk and eat pepperoni pizza. We came to the conclusion that we both hated our fucking jobs and neither one of us should go back. But just to be assholes we would both use the same excuse for not coming into work, and then we would call in the night before we were supposed to be there. Our first excuse was to be that we both had hemorrhoids and couldn't make it in on Monday to slave all day in the Georgia sun for meager wages. I was leaving town soon anyways so I was down for it. Sunday night rolled around and I fell asleep and didn't wake up until noon on Monday. I called Johnny around 6 p.m. to see if he had called in. That pussy was talking shit the whole time, and he still went to work. I never called in or actually ever quit, I just never went back. I guess I won't ask for a reference for a little while from old John W. Ayers Plumbing Company.

+++

Infested

I have an infested body

Allergic reactions

And chemical imbalances

Produce red bumps

On my chest and arms and legs

Neck and back

Creams and pills

Do nothing

For my infested body

There is no cure

And no treatment

Patience my boy

Patience

Of which I have none

And scratch the infestation

Thus

Just making it worse

Red

And scaly and itching

Come share

My infested body

Don't worry

It's not contagious

Come closer

+++

She walked up to me as I was getting out of my car.

"Hey Brett how are you?" she asked.

"I'm a little hung over but I'll survive."

I guess she noticed that I had a look of confusion on my face.

"You don't remember me do you?"

"I have to admit that you look familiar but I can't remember where I know you from."

"I know that's bad, but I'm a fucking drunk and my memory is really horrible."

"Fuck you asshole!"

"Damn baby what did I do?"

"I'm sorry I don't remember you, but it's not my fault."

"I blame the PBR."

"That's really fucked up Brett. I'm glad I meant so much to you and made such an impression on you."

"I met you a few months ago in a bar."

"Do you remember me now Brett?"

"Sorry, I'm still not remembering anything."

"Well we made out in the bathroom."

"You said you loved me."

"Oh yea, now I remember you."

"How the hell you been?"

+++

I sit here in deep thought. I'm alone as always. I revel in it. Not a human being on this Earth could walk through my bedroom door and cure my disease. There is no one that could fill the void and cure this loneliness. It's always been there and always will be. It keeps me away from people, and that's a majority of the time a good thing. I know how they are out there, weak, stupid, and soulless. Here alone I'm happy so why fuck up a good thing?

+++

I was bored in the shower today so I peed on myself for no reason at all. I had to soap my legs up again after I did it. It wasn't bad; I might do it more often now. It's all about efficiency people. Why use a toilet when I have a shower? It's bigger anyways and I don't have to worry about shaking afterwards.

+++

Lust

The worst of all the seven deadly sins

Forcing lies

From us all

Actions regretted

In a haze of alcohol

Clouded memories

Rats

Skewering over a chunk of cheese

In the dirty corners

And the sewers of life

Where we belong

+++

I felt like killing myself today. It would really start Christmas out with a bang. Everyone would be bummed out, what a present!

+++

I stumbled in drunker than usual that night. I gazed the crowd that had infiltrated my bar. They were the rich and beautiful people of Myrtle Beach. I noticed that in the parking lot there were more expensive cars than usual, so I guess I can back up my observations with that, and the lack of people drinking domestic beer. I sat down next to a very beautiful girl that I had never seen before this night and said "Hey, you look just like a bitch I fucked a while ago." Her jaw dropped onto the table and she got up and left. I sat there for a few minutes longer alone with my PBR. I don't remember much after that, not even how the hell I got home. When I woke up the next day my car was parked at a forty-five degree angle in the parking lot of my apartment complex.

+++

I'm sick as fuck in London. I thought I was going to hack up a lung while I was riding the Tube. People stared at me so I moved between cars to avoid their attention. It's gloomy and miserable here just like I imagined it to be from listening to all those Smiths records. I walked past Parliament and Big Ben. People were yelling and protesting the war in Iraq. I walked past them and I glanced at their homemade signs and smiled. I leaned against an old stone wall as rain falls hard on my head. I leaned over and cough up blood. I spit into the Thames River. I light a cigarette and keep walking.

+++

Alien man walking

Amongst them

No one can see it

But I can feel it

Another planet

Is where I belong

Human flesh I'm covered

Alien man talking

Mind is a thought and language

They can't even understand

Algebraic equations

Unsolved

The numbers make no sense at all

Alien man isolation

The answer to the impossible question

+++

The only thing keeping me going at the moment are memories of past actions that are almost long forgotten in my mind. SEX! There it is all the time lurking in my frontal lobe and rising in my pants. Furious masturbation can only calm the need for SEX! Two hours later and it's there in my head once again. SEX! It calls out to me in movies or even on the Discovery Channel after I watched two antelopes fucking in the Pacific Northwest. SEX! It won't go away. There's nothing I can do about. I sit at home alone. You can't get SEX! there you fucking idiot. It's the one guaranteed place on the planet that you cannot get SEX! at, and you know that. What am I to do? Where can I get SEX! right now? I scramble through long forgotten phone numbers of girls so I can get SEX! from them and then leave. SEX! Go out and look for it. Go to your favorite bar and seek it out with a passion. No, it's not that sort of meat market kind of place, just losers and typical drunks like me. I need to find a new bar so I can find SEX! easily and with no strings attached. Maybe some girl who just broke up with her boyfriend will be there and will be looking for rebound SEX! or maybe some ugly girl no one wants and is as desperate as I am will be there looking for SEX! The only places like that are some shitty dance clubs where they play bad music that I hate. Those kinds of girls don't like you and would never want to have SEX! with you anyway. What if I go there and stand in a corner alone and drink over priced beer and no SEX! is available to me? I'll be right back where I started, but with less money and feeling even more pathetic then I was before. SEX! I need you right now from anyone I can get it from. Until I find SEX! My small collection of Juggs Magazines will have to get me through these barren times in Myrtle Beach.

+++

The days and the nights pass me by slowly, creeping up on me and then retreating before any sort of enjoyment could be had. Day by day I sit here alone and apathetic to the world moving rapidly outside of my door. I watch it from a dirty window inside of the city. I've got to turn it on if I have to go out there again. I prepare myself daily for the oncoming storm known as that fucking jungle outside of my dirty window. Nothing can prepare you for its brutality and leech like structure set up to destroy you and any humanity that might be left inside of you. Fast food turns slowly rotting and attracting microscopic organisms beyond the view of my eye. There are knocks at my door that I don't get off of the couch to answer. Phone calls never returned and soon no more phone calls from those people out there. I still sit here in an uncomfortable black chair as the seasons pass slowly and bad movies become worse. Conversations I don't miss and the human touch I have long forgotten, and the need for human contact has diminished. Those days earlier mentioned have now turned into months, and yet I still sit here observing the world from a dirty window inside of the city.

+++

Cigarette lit

Smoke fills the air and disappears quickly

I look down and notice

Cum stains on my floor

I'm pathetic and can't even do that right

It's not rocket science or anything

But cumming perfectly on a rolled up piece of Charmin

Is harder than you girls might think

No, I'm not going to clean it up

Eventually it will harden and crust

And be a reminder to those new tenants

That yes

Brett Stout did reside here

+++

New York City, winter 2004, I was walking near Times Square today when I noticed a large perfect pile of white vomit lying right in the middle of the street. I stopped and admired it for a second. Now that was perfection I thought to myself. I pulled out my crappy disposable camera and snapped a few pictures of this perfect pile of white vomit. People stopped to look at me. I just nodded and kept taking my pictures. What a perfect metaphor for this city.

+++

We were friends for a long time. I remember the first time that I saw you. That moment is burned into my brain forever. We were fast friends the first time we talked at work. You were the only person that didn't yell at me or correct me on something I was doing wrong. You took pity on a lowly eighteen year old punk rock dishwasher and I appreciated it. Kind and the restaurant industry don't go hand in hand, especially in the back of the kitchen. I remember that you hated the job as much as I did, but you had the sense to quit before I did. I kept hammering it out for another year somehow. We grew apart when you left the job. Conversations, funny stories, and drunken nights became fewer and farther apart. You fell into a bad crowd. I tried to warn you about them but my words went unnoticed. I remember that summer day you came to the back of the kitchen and asked me for some food. I fixed you some chicken fingers and fries and gave you some of my cigarettes. You looked pretty bad. Your beauty was hidden under the dirt and foul smell you were wearing. I heard crazy stories about you from time to time. My friend Joe even said you gave him a hand job for ten bucks over in Candler Park. I was sad to hear that. I remember the last time I saw you walking down Moreland Ave. I wondered where you were headed and what you were doing, but I didn't stop to ask. I now regret that. A week later I heard you were found dead in some ghetto apartment complex on the Southside of Atlanta.

+++

I went to the grocery store today for the first time in forever. I held out for as long as I could. I waited in line and had the ladies at the deli cut two large bags of shaved smoked turkey. They seemed pissed that I asked for it shaved. I grabbed Doritos, nacho Goldfish, and a bag of frosted animal cookies as well. My arms were full as I hit the checkout line. The old lady started scanning my items. I walked over towards the little debit card swiper which was near the register. I went for my wallet but I noticed that it wasn't there. "Fuck," was the only word that came to mind. I lied and told the lady that had I left my wallet in the car and I would be right back. I ran out to my car started it up and got the hell out of there. It looks like I will be avoiding Piggly Wiggly for a while.

+++

The neighbors never shut up. They yell and scream and make asses of themselves. Random fireworks go off during the day. I hear stupid things come out of their mouths afterwards. When they have their rap music turned up really loud I try and ignore it, but I can't really. I've been thinking about buying a handgun lately. I would walk over there on a nice Sunday afternoon and shoot whoever opened the door in the face. I'm a nice guy so I would only take out the knee caps of whoever else was there at the time. I would then walk back over to my place and cook a frozen pizza and watch some TV in peace for once.

+++

The walk of shame

Hell, it has even happened to me a few times

Hoping to God

That no one saw me

Leave that fat girl's apartment

In the morning

Holding my head in shame

Damn you PBR

Damn you

The booze is wearing off

But my cock is still hard

From the past night's sex

Door opens

I get in

Speeding past

Brick apartments

Home

In a few short minutes

+++

"That son of a bitch called me into his office today."

"What did he want this time?"

"Nothing really, he just bitched at me a little for being late almost everyday."

"He said I needed to make a decision on my future with the company."

"He said that if I was late again that I shouldn't even bother coming in."

"I think he's full of shit though."

"Like one of those scared straight programs back in school."

"Ha-ha, yea I remember going down to Fulton Country jail and this big black motherfucker said that he was going to kick our asses if we didn't straighten up."

"He was full of shit though, he just did it for an extra desert at dinner everyday probably."

"I mean how hard is it to scare a bunch of privileged white kids anyways?"

"I'm sick of this fucking job man, so if he wants to fire me I don't even care."

"I'll just collect unemployment if he ever does fire me."

"I'll be a bum for a month and not do jack shit but lie around my apartment and jerk off and get drunk."

"He wants me to quit I can tell it."

"You think so Brett?"

"I wouldn't give him the satisfaction of me quitting."

"That fucking cocksucker!"

"Are you going to start showing up on time?"

"Fuck it, hell no, just to piss him off I'm going be twice as late as I usually am tomorrow."

"It's not like I haven't been fired before or something."

"If he does fire me tomorrow I'm going to piss on his BMW before I leave."

"That will teach him, that son of a bitch."

"Hand me another Dixie will you there Johnny?"

+++

Stupid fucking white women, only they could be that materialistic and vain. Chase those celebrities and athletes. It seems like high school bullshit never ended for you. Snort that coke and somehow remain beautiful, yet I'm the only one that can see how ugly and unhappy you are deep inside. Fuck as many guys as you can looking for happiness, but the only thing you will have to show is a loose vagina. Sucker one of your guys to pay a plastic surgeon to tighten your loose pussy for you. Life's great when you can be a whore and not have any of those consequences anymore. Now if only they could make a pill to get rid of some of those Sexually Transmitted Diseases, then life would be just peachy.

+++

I wake up from my nightmare and wonder where the fuck I am. I can't sleep. I just lay there and sweat in the middle of the summer lying in my bed. I stumble to the bathroom and take a piss. I have a hard on so I piss all over the floor. I try and aim but it does no good. I leave the piss on the floor and lie back down. I'm scared of sleeping. I know what happens if I do. She is haunting me still.

+++

I look at it with apprehension

Oval shapes of pink moving while hyenas

Are laughing in the distance

Body of water a few steps away while flesh burns

Under the mid-day sky

A hang over stained wreck sits while a silhouette moves closer

And closer

Confusion hits while the Clash song

Should I Stay or Should I Go plays in my head

+++

A midget wearing a crown of thorns straps me down. He walks around me and fiddles with tools placed on his little metal tray. He pokes my arm with his needle of death and tapes it down. Mysterious green fluid jets into my veins. It fills me with laughter and ease. He grabs a dull fork and begins stabbing me in the chest. He laughs as I cry for mercy from my chair. Jab after jab, each hurts worse than the one before. His arm begins to tire after chipping away on my rib cage. He takes a break and tells me a joke while he slowly puffs away on a cigarette. His giraffe-headed assistant urges him to finish. He grabs the same dull fork and goes back to work on my rib cage. Blood has stained the chair and I can now hear it dripping on the floor. After another forty-five minutes of jabbing he is done and lays the dull fork down on the little tray. He reaches in with his childlike hands and pulls out my meaty bloody heart. He looks at it with amazement and then throws it on the floor. The giraffe-headed assistant picks it up and places it in a Ziploc bag and then tosses it in the large receptacle that's in the corner of the room. The midget grabs a few cans of Play-Doh from a cabinet and begins shaping a new heart for me. A few minutes pass as I lay in agony. He soon has formed me a new heart like structure and places it in my chest cavity. He gives me a Lucifer like grin as his little beady eyes light up with excitement. He grabs a box of old shoe strings and begins sewing me back up. He yanks the last one tight and ties it in a knot. He pats me the shoulder and says I took it great. The giraffe-headed assistant unlocks my chains and I rise up. He says next time be more careful. I hand him a wad of cash and then I disappear into the shadows.

+++

Her long red nails dig into my back

Through my black t-shirt

Her strength is incredible

I must be fucking her pretty good

That's a nice change I guess

Her leg is stuck in the front seatbelt

As I pound away on her

Sweat begins to pour from my head and onto my face

Burning my eyes

Pounding as the minutes tick away

In the dark empty parking lot

Of an empty breakfast buffet restaurant

I finally can't take it anymore

Her pussy feels too good

Too wet

Like silk or nirvana

I tense up as I empty

My cum inside her

I rest my head on her shoulders

And kiss her neck

I pull myself from inside of her

As cum drips from her pussy

And onto my brown dirty

Cracked backseat

+++

My girlfriend had the abortion on Friday night. I hid the little alien-like body in my Dukes of Hazzard lunchbox after she gave birth to it. I forgot that I did it though after I got drunk later that night. I walked into the lunch room that following Monday. I expected to see my usual chicken sandwich, bag of Doritos, and my Sprite. They were not there though. Instead, the little alien-like body made of eggs and sperm was in my lunchbox. I went to the lunch line and ordered two plain pieces of white bread. I sat back down and laid the little body on my two pieces of bland white bread. I added a little dash of salt and pepper as well as some ketchup and then I bit into it. The sandwich was a little dry, but it actually tasted better than the sloppy joe I had here last week.

+++

Last night a drunken piggy back ride went horribly wrong. Sorry baby, I didn't mean to drop you in the parking lot. I think I took the blunt of the force the pavement offered us. I tumbled over like the Twin Towers did on that cold Tuesday morning. This is what happens when I'm drunk. It was a good idea at the time, but not so much now as I try and clear my head and pick the gravel out of my hands and knees. I have a nice new pretty gash on my right kneecap.

No need for a Band-Aid or peroxide though. That whiskey I put on it should do the job just fine. Next time baby, no piggy back rides when I'm drunk, ok?

+++

I walk into a truck stop off of Interstate 75. The brunette waitress who is covered in grease comes over and asks me what I would like to drink. I replied "Is the piss fresh today?" She states "Yea, I haven't even made it yet but it should be nice and warm." She disappears for a few minutes while I browse the grease stained menu. She returns to the table with a large clear glass. She then puts her left leg up on the other side of the booth and brings the glass up to her vagina and begins to piss. She fills the glass up only three quarters of the way. She waits a few seconds and then spits out a few more squirts. She hands the glass to me and I begin chugging away. It's halfway gone and I wipe the excess off on my sleeve. She puts her leg down and asks me what I'll have to eat. I say "Three scrambled eggs, bacon, and toast please." She scribbles it down on her little pad and proceeds into the kitchen.

+++

I'm covered in medals from Vietnam. I am naked. They are not pinned into any jacket or shirt but into my flesh. I bleed profusely as I stand at attention. I salute the flag as I fall to my knees. I beg God for forgiveness, but no one answers. Little Asian children pelt me with rocks as I lie in a pool of my own blood, shit, and piss.

+++

God touched me today

In a special place

He made offerings of candy

To take a ride

So I did

My mom called the cops

He's now doing 25 to life in San Quentin

Tossing the salad of a large black man

In cell 329

+++

I walked into a gas station the other day. I usually despise taking a shit in public but this time it couldn't be helped. Traffic was congested and there was no fucking way I was making it home this time. I held my ass together as tight as I could until I thought I felt a little bit of shit come out of my asshole and touch my underwear. An Amoco gas station was my only choice. I had stopped there before, but I had never used the bathroom. Of course, when I walked in the store the men's bathroom was locked. I didn't know whether it was one of those bathrooms I might need a key for or if someone was in there. I leaned against the outer door of the freezer and decided to wait it out for a second before I asked the clerk what the deal was. I heard the blower come on and then the door opened. A large black man hurried out and I went it. Lucky for me I guess he just had to piss since there wasn't a shit smell in the air as I walked in. Piss drops were on the seat and there was no more toilet paper so I just huddled over the seat after I had pulled my pants down. There was no time for rational thoughts of why there was no more toilet paper or how to possibly acquire some before taking the shit itself. My ass just dropped a load of squirts and ass water that burned as is came out of me. One huge lunge and it was over. A feeling of euphoria rushed over me and I was at peace with the world once again. A few nasty shitty farts later and then my mind turned to the problem at hand. There was no toilet paper! Fuck me! All the ideas of what my options were flashed through my head. I could just not wipe my ass at all. I could use my hand, or I could possibly even use my shirt. Then the idea hit me. Why not take off my pants and use my underwear as toilet paper. My Clash shirt was too important and cost a lot more than a pair of Classic Hanes underwear. I slowly and carefully eased off my camo shorts and slipped off my shoes and tried not to stand in the pool of urine that was on the floor for too long. My underwear eased off without too many problems. My light blue underwear slowly turned shit brown after several strokes back and forth. It was a small price to pay for a clean ass.

+++

We went miniature golfing around 5 p.m.

We ate tacos around 6:30

The movie lasted from 8-10

You were sucking my cock around 10:11 in my car

I took you home around 10:45

You called me at 10:57

I didn't answer

You called again at 11:03

I still didn't answer

You called and left a message this time at 12:34

I listened but didn't call you back

You called and left another message at 1:56 a.m.

You said that it would be your last one

You didn't call me again after that night

You told all your friends I was an inconsiderate asshole

You were right

+++

Disgusting fat women are standing near the dressing rooms. Their chubby legs jiggle with every stride they take. I watch them as they try on clothes way too small for them. They stretch them out and then put them back on the racks for the next consumer to buy. They dig through a huge crate of discount movies. They celebrate at the Columbus like discovery of Rambo II and Major League. High fives are in order for finding thought provoking films like that. They jiggle along and they push their carts some more. I overhear them talking now, bitching about their shitty kids and talking about what great deals there are in here today. I follow them at a distance. They jiggle through the food isles picking up dinner for their little brats I guess. Then they jiggle towards the long checkout line. They grab mind altering magazines like People and TV Guide to entertain them during the wait. I take a quick left and then disappear. They are still flipping through magazines as I lose sight of them.

+++

The streets of Baghdad are cracked and broken

Streams of blood run cold

We're here to save you we swear

While maimed and dead brown children

Lay in agony

Imperialist corporations smile with deceit

Just another border of consumerism

And cheap labor

Let the lower classes

Do our dirty work and salute the flag

McDonalds and Wal Mart are a part of

Every civilized society

We will count our billions as always

The same as in Cuba, The Philippines, Guam

And let's not forget Vietnam

+++

Is Jesus' middle name Dale now? I must have missed something along the way. In every gas station and on the back of large trucks in the South, Dale still reigns free it seems. His image graces the likes of lighters, cup holders, stickers, hats, license plate frames, pens, and assortment of other items that you can find at truck stops. He is the real redneck Jesus it seems to me. Under large mustache and Southern accent, the god of driving a car around in an oval circle embraces and saves all of the little trailer park children, but not if they're red, yellow, or black. Dale, Dale, where have you gawn? Our lives are moot and lacking in significance without seeing you ride around that oval circle 300 times on Sunday afternoons after we eat our ten piece bucket of KFC fried chicken. I can imagine rednecks saving paychecks until they have enough money to go down to the local psychic to talk to the spirit of Dale. Maybe garnering relationship advice or lotto numbers since they're already there talking to the almighty Dale. It's no wonder these people bought into the concept of a free Iraq or believe George Bush is a decent god fearing human being. Anyone that admires or misses a guy who drove a car around an oval circle for a living have to be stupid as shit in my mind. Dale, Dale, where have you gawn?

+++

Sand in my crotch

Behavior

Lice feast upon a woman's yeast infection

Masochistic behavior

Cum drips from her slightly pink eye

Of masochistic behavior

A bayonet enters a soldier's midsection

Joys of masochistic behavior

Herpes blisters fester on a testicle sac

The joys of masochistic behavior

A young child is decapitated by a Honda Civic

Oh the joys of masochistic behavior

Brain matter festers on a dirt floor

The

An asshole is stretched on a drunken Saturday night

The joys

Urination enters her mouth

The joys of

A black man swings from a branch in Alabama

The joys of masochistic

Colostomy bag birthday balloons pop

The joys of masochistic behavior

A self-inflicted gunshot wound at the end of a day

Oh the joys of masochistic behavior

Swedish girls eat shit for hard currency

Joy

While AIDS gnaws away at a face

Joy

Jesus is raped in a Catholic Church shower

Joy

Everyday life is an alluring tragic thing

Joy

+++

It seems like America is being swept up in a rampant nationalism these days.
Everyday when I get the newspaper I read about more killings in Iraq and
Afghanistan. It's depressing to me. This is a bad time to be alive and to grow
up. I wish we had minded our own business and the let the U.N. handle things
for a little longer. I wish no one was dying, but I can't weep for soldiers when
they die. Odds are they did something along the way to deserve what they get.
It's a bad situation all around. The thoughts of traveling the world and getting a
free education are tempting to poor kids like me. I mean fuck, I almost joined
the military on many occasions when I was in a desperate situation. I'm glad I
didn't of course, but it was very tempting. I knew I would be put in situations
where I would have to kill fucking people that I had never met and had done
nothing to me personally. The thought of blowing an eight-year-old's head off
in the name of "Freedom" is something that I could not be morally alright with.
Yet, many of these supposed "Heroes" do just that and worse and are rewarded
for it. Granted, anytime a human being is put into a situation of life and death,
most would kill anyone they had to, to stay alive, that's just human nature. But
to make martyrs and heroes of them is something I will not participate in.
Frankly, we should collect the heads of every woman and child killed in Iraq
and walk into Congress, The Senate, and The White House and dump their
rotting heads all over their plush carpets. The sight of this would force our
representatives to stop the war immediately. Every person who voted to go to
war would feel so guilty and haunted by this site they would perform a mass
suicide on the White House Lawn. George Bush would not be allowed to
commit suicide though, that would be too easy. He would instead be flown to
Baghdad and be forced to apologize door to door to every family that lost a
child for his bullshit cause. He would then be decapitated and the children of

Iraq would play soccer with his head while lines of people waited in line to defecate on his rotting corpse.

+++

Brown and green mucus flows

From my body and into

A little red plastic cup

That I keep near me

On my computer desk

I hack and cough like a man

Fifty years my elder

I look in the cup and spot small slices and bits of my

Right and left lung

They now are dead and will spend the rest of their days floating

In Juicy Juice residue

In a small red plastic cup

I cough so hard that I almost

Choke

My eyes turn red

As I grasp for breath

And my nose fills up with snot

I light another cigarette and pop small white pills

In honor of my dead lung

That now floats in a small red plastic cup

That sits near me

On my computer desk

+++

My eyes are closed and my body tenses up. A few strokes and I feel the cum churning in my balls. I pull my cock out of you and I try and make it from lying on my knees to leaning over you so I can cum on your face. You take my cock in your mouth and begin to suck on my head. You aren't very good at it but I don't say anything to you about it. I take my cock in my hand and stroke until I feel the cum churning once again in my balls. I feel my body tense up once again. I can feel it moving now. A few more strokes and it will be out. Fuck! It shoots out like a rocket on the 4th of July and onto your face. Some of it slides down onto your eyelid. I sort of hope some of it goes in your eye before I get off of you. I wait and pretend like I have a hard time moving before you stumble into the bathroom and grab my towel to clean your face off with.

+++

I often find myself cooking ninety-nine cent pizzas by myself in my apartment. Outside my front door is nothing but assholes and jerk-offs so I try not to open it too much these days. I've learned my lesson. Anytime I deal with them it always goes bad and I end of disappointed, so why even bother with them anymore? I would rather be unshaven and smelling of B.O. and wearing the same pants for weeks at a time. Who needs any of it? I'm the only one fucking evolving around here. The rest don't have a clue.

+++

Pussy

Cunt

Guts

Taco

Beaver

Cooter

Box

Snatch

Clam

Twat

Slit

Meat pocket

Whatever you want to call it

Doesn't matter to me

I had forgotten what it smells like

What it feels like

What it tastes like

How wet it is

What my fingers feel when I put them

Inside of her

And then pull them out and lick them

The way it parts and moves and looks

When my cock is moving in and out of it

I forgot how crazy it makes me

And how I would lie, cheat, or steal

Just to get some of it

Fuck cold fusion or smart bombs

Pussy

Cunt

Guts

Taco

Beaver

Cooter

Box

Snatch

Clam

Twat

Slit

Meat pocket

Is the real technology that I still marvel at

+++

Sometimes I think hope is the worst affliction than one can have. There is always that little voice in my head telling me that there's a chance that I can have and get what I want eventually. If I stay in the war long enough eventually victory will be at hand. But rarely is this the case. Hope, my friend, is a bitch.

+++

I was sitting on a curb while some shitty punk rock band was playing inside the small venue on Memorial Avenue. Summertime in Atlanta is so fucking hot and humid, and today is no exception. Even as the sun goes down sweat pours down my face. There's no air conditioning in the club so you can only take it inside for around twenty minutes at a time. I walk over to the ghetto gas station down the street and get a 40oz of Budweiser. I walk back to the club and my previous seat is still there so I sit back down. I stomp on the massive amounts of ants on the ground between sips of my beer. The band that was playing finishes up and people start coming outside in massive droves. I just sit and watch all the punks complain about how hot it is and how awesome the band was. A girl with a red Mohawk sits down next to me. Out of nowhere she hits me in the head with her fists three or four times. I grab her hands and I ask her what the fuck she thinks she is doing. Some of her other punk rock friends come over and take her away. I never found out why that crazy girl with the mohawk wanted to beat me up. The Atlanta heat makes people insane it seems.

+++

I don't give a shit about my job anymore. I want to be fired. It makes me sick to see that I bust my ass everyday for my ungrateful Eurotrash owners. They don't deserve to own a business. I just need a break that's all. I will be something one day maybe if given a chance. I don't know what I want to do though. Anything is better than coming home everyday covered in sweat and having chicken and fish guts on my shoes.

+++

It's judgment time. Either I tell them to fuck off and give me my paycheck or I work another month and quit.

+++

She got mad when I called her a fucking drunken whore

It's true though

Every time I go to the bar for a drink

You're there

Like a barstool

With a pulse

Every night going home

With someone new

Dragging yourself back in every night

Looking for a new victim

I watch in enjoyment

Every night

Sipping my beer slowly

+++

White women are the worst. You said you were into nasty sex, but when I tried to fuck your ass or jerk off in your face you said you weren't into it. I laughed and called you a "Fucking poser."

+++

I remember it was around Christmas. I heard on the news that one suburban housewife punched another suburban housewife in Wal Mart over some shitty toy their miserable little bastard children were screaming for. When they get out of jail they should go home to their little houses in the suburbs and get the family gun out and shoot their kids while they sleep. Then they should take a swig of Zima and then eat the gun themselves. I would like to turn on the news and hear about that instead.

+++

Thunder strikes outside my window

Rain pellets crash against my door

The smell of sex

Is still in the air

It is silent now though

My legs ache with every move

In fact every part of me aches

With every move

The consequences of the fucking I guess

Getting older as well

I wash the sheets covered in stains

And sweat from last night

They hadn't been washed in six months

So I figured it was time

+++

I had gone away to my Mom's house for Christmas. I had five days off from work which was awesome. Doing construction work in the dead of winter was no pleasant experience let me tell you. I came back on a Sunday evening from my Mom's house in Virginia. I walked up the wobbly narrow stairs of my old shitty apartment building. When I got to the top I noticed that my door was cracked open. I knew I would have never left that door open if I was going out of town. I walked in and looked around to see what the fuck had happened while I was away. The apartment was empty. What little I had some lowlife motherfucker had stolen. Gone was my forty dollar TV set I bought from a homeless guy. Gone was my guitar my friend had stolen but given to me. They had also taken my crappy old VCR and all of my porno tapes along with it. Goodbye "Cum Swapping Sluts #3" and "Anal Fever Whores." Those were my two favorites. Why couldn't they have just left those two for me? I guess it doesn't matter since I don't have a VCR to watch them on anyways. They had even taken my rarely cleaned microwave. There's a nice surprise when those fuckheads open it I guess. I went into the bathroom to take a piss and one of them had even taken a shit in the toilet and not flushed it. I pushed the handle down and of course it stopped-up the toilet. I went for the plunger which usually sat between the toilet and my shower that lacked hot water, but of course they had taken that as well. I just went and sat on my raggedy futon in complete silence knowing someone had gotten the better of me and there wasn't shit I could do about it. Congratulations, you bastards!

+++

Your blue eyes stare at me as you wear an evil little smile. I keep stroking my cock with the shampoo in the little bottle with the hotel imprint on it. My cock is burning from it. The pain almost keeps me from cumming. My balls tighten up and my cum shoots all over your face and chin. I watch it drip onto your huge tits and you grab my cock and suck out the rest. You say it tastes great and I ask if you want the cum that has gathered on your large rack. I take my hand and get it up as best as I can. I put my fingers down your throat as you lick my cum from them. I light a cigarette as my cock goes limp.

+++

A sea-a-wash with gray stone strip malls

Convenience and boredom

What a trip

The land of the free

The home of the brave cheap Chinese goods

The bloated sound of large white asses

Sitting on tan Hummer leather

The stock market is up

And the masses are down

Knees bent honoring our rag paper gods of despair

Erectile Dysfunction

Happens even worse on Columbus Day

A house of cheap whores

Foundations of sand

Oh how we must sit back now and marvel at our greatness

+++

I threw my Television set off of the balcony today. I'd had enough of the lies and bullshit for one lifetime. I'm just one man trying to keep the modern world at bay.

+++

My fear is not of mass murderers, child molesters, or even rapists. Those have been a constant through the ages and are not going to disappear as long as human beings exist on this Earth. My fear is of the fat white suburban housewives driving minivans, shopping at Wal Mart, and breeding the next army of mindless drones. All the while complaining about niggers, gas prices, and how the coach of little Johnny's baseball team is an idiot for not playing little Johnny more. Now that scares the fucking shit out of me.

+++

I was cutting a piece of tile today. I bent down to try and a make a precise cut that I needed. The tile cutting machine jammed and spat the piece of tile right back in my face. It didn't really hurt, but from the amount of blood gushing everywhere I knew something was really bad. I looked at my face from the reflection on the front door. The tile had split my face in two from the inside of my nose and all the way to my bottom lip. At a closer glance it looked like I had developed a large vagina on my face. I poked it a few times with my nasty stained hands. I went inside and had my boss look at it. He was freaking out and insisted on taking me to the hospital. I said "Don't worry about it, everything is fine." I did ask for a towel or something to stop the bleeding. He talked me into going to one of those walk-in clinics instead of the hospital. I waited for about half an hour and then the pretty blonde nurse led me back into a dim lit doctor's office. He took a look at me and told me to lie down on the table. He put a large gauze pad over my face. He said he was going to have to give me numerous shots in my already busted face to numb the pain. It was the most painful thing ever done to me actually. I tried to be as tough as I could, but tears ran out of my eyes anyways. After around eight pokes he was done and put the cap back on the needle. The doctor then proceeded with the stitching. He took his time and I laid there for what felt like an eternity. I got up and looked in the mirror when he was done. I had a plethora of little black stitches going vertically down my face. I said "Hey doc how many stitches did you put in?" He replied "Quite a few, twenty-three I think." I love it, twenty-three more added to my collection. I want a thousand by the time these bastards are done with me.

+++

My baby left me and moved to California. Most people think that dreams come true there, but I know better. That's where in fact that dreams go to die. Stay here in the South baby where things make sense and where people still open car doors for girls and say yes ma'am. Los Angeles is full of fake fucking people. There's nothing genuine about the place or them. I like it here where there's normal people and normal towns. It might be a little boring but that's ok. At least I know where I stand in this place. Anything is better than being around a bunch of actors and models and the leeches that follow them around kissing their asses. I hope you find what you're looking for out there. Maybe one day you will come back to me.

+++

Freedom spells oppression

What freedom I ask

The freedom to choose where I buy my

Cheap non-nutritional processed food from

Burger King or McDonalds

Now that's freedom in all it's withered glory

The American Dream is dead

For all but a few

White men in suits walking the streets

Of New York and D.C.

We're all just pawns and consumers

In the corporate game of life

A game of Risk

Which I for one don't wish to play

+++

I tried to be a nice guy and walk you to your car. You stumbled the entire way but I kept my arm on your shoulder to steady your every step. I thought this was a chance for me to be a nice fucking guy for once and do something decent for someone. We were looking for your blue Honda Accord. After scouring the parking lot for ten minutes and making several wrong judgments on similar looking cars, we finally found your piece of shit blue Honda Accord. After watching you not be able to get the key into the lock after many tries, I offered to do it for you. I got the key in on the first try. All my years of drinking and driving were paying off already. You sat down in the front seat of your car. After fumbling around in your purse looking for your cigarettes, you asked me to help out. I grabbed the large brown purse and on the first try found your cigarettes and lighter. I handed them to you and you lit it after fumbling with your lighter for a few seconds. I felt bad. I suggested that you just hop in the backseat and take a nap until you sobered up. You weren't hearing that at all. You said not to worry about it. Then two seconds later you said that you probably couldn't drive home after all. You said to let you call a few friends and see if anyone could come pick you up. I said ok and lit a cigarette as you fumbled through numbers on your phone looking for someone to call. I overhear the first conversation and whoever you were talking to was at work. I overheard a second conversation and no luck once again. This starts wearing on me. I was standing there smoking and freezing to death without a jacket. I once again suggest that you get in the backseat and sleep it off, and once again you say no way. Finally, my patience runs out and my original good decent act goes entirely bad. I stand there a few minutes more and then I say I need to head home and take a shit. I figured this would be a believable story. You said that you would just drive home. I gave in and said ok and waved goodbye as you swerved out of the parking lot.

+++

Burning clocks fuel my late nights

Freedom reigns from large red veins

Searing steaks and red tablecloths placed on wood

GHB a white girl's dream

Where did it all go wrong for me?

Questions posed but never answered

Fields of depression are grown

Cared for under a mid-summer sun

Stalks of alienation are burning

While tractor tires are turning under Georgia clay

Where did it all go wrong for me?

Violet faces spew untold truths

Russian gulags made of glass

Rats and old men chase bare chested women

Together a lie is birthed

Developing cancer and neon signs

Where did it all go wrong for me?

A pavement walk that leads me in a dead end

Consistent revolution from both church and sand

Hourglasses overflow

Time wasted and masturbation well received

Glowing reviews of the next great sin

Where did it all go wrong for me?

+++

No fucking wonder kids are killing kids these days and mass neurosis is being diagnosed. Look at the fucking example that's being set. War is the answer and Dr. Phil keeps talking bullshit. Who's to blame? It's easy for the baby boomers to blame music, movies, and video games, but we all know those are easy bullshit excuses and scapegoats. The blame instead lies on you, the parents. You fucked us up. Your greed was a catalyst for our demise and destructive behavior. Finally take some responsibility and admit it. While Mom and Dad both worked all day and night to give us this "Better life than they had" fairy tale, little Johnny was being raised by MTV reality shows, smoking crack, and stroking your gun. So look no further than yourselves Mom and Dad when looking for a scapegoat after the next school shooting or overdose. If you had taken the time to get to know us and listen to us maybe this could have been avoided.

+++

Clubbing baby seals just for kicks

Brains are for consuming

Not rationale thoughts

Freedom rings but never at my door

Barefoot and pregnant with wolverine twins

Streams of sperm from which the animals drink

Inauspicious neighbors are dead on my front lawn

Kleptomaniacs boil their spleens

From hot plates bought and paid for at Wal Mart

Euphoria plagues

And the Sahara freezes

The end of humanity is a glorious scene

+++

Insanity is something most will never know. It's either never there from the start, there too much, or something you gradually grow into. I'm one of those gradual lunatics. The older I get the more fucking crazier I get it seems. I couldn't fucking care anymore, life lived in normalcy is something I don't know much about anyways. It's like being rich; if you've never been then you're ignorant enough to know you think you're not missing much. That's my story. I plant my flag in the extreme now. Fuck trying to be normal, it was an impossible task to begin with. Coming to terms with being a fucked up human being sometimes takes a little time and patience.

+++

My girl's a junky now

From love to heroin

Coke and double vodkas

The love disappeared

But the habit didn't

She trying to kick it

In rehab

She calls me from time to time

Collect

I always accept it

On a dare

She's a conformist now

Group therapy

Eating pudding and basket weaving

My little junky girl

Purple veins and a red swollen nose

An American tragedy

Some might say

+++

My friend from a town nearby was headed over to see me that night. She never showed up. I called her phone a few times but all I got was the machine. That same annoying answering machine message over and over and over again until I had it memorized even down to the distinct pauses in her voice. I found out a week later she got busted by the cops for DUI and simple possession. She's still in jail I hear, but I keep calling. Maybe one day she will pick up.

+++

I only have three more days of work left and then I'm quitting. I hate this job with a passion now. Any job I have for longer than six months ends up being this way. I get fed up and bored of the sheer mundane routine of it. The hot stinking stressful kitchen doesn't help either. The white tickets printing out never end. On weekends, the tickets overflow into the floor and curl up like some kind of paper snake. I don't know why I did it, but just for spite I walked into the freezer when no one was around and I put my dick and balls and part of my ass into the next batch of mashed potatoes. All my anxiety and stress melted away once my large sack and hairy ass was firmly planted in those soft potatoes. The only negative was having to work the rest of the night with the mashed potatoes all over my crotch. But when I got home and took a shower I felt it was well worth the effort to do it. Anyone who has ever worked in the back of a kitchen has thought about it at one time or another, but it's a rarity to actually make it happen. This is the insanity that happens when one ceases to give a shit about a job.

+++

Wal Mart is the perfect metaphor for everything that is wrong with America. It's crowded, full of inept obese people, cheap, and miserable.

+++

The last time my Mom took me to a theme park

Was the last time she ever did

Six Flags in Atlanta

On a hot summer day

My friend dared me to jump off

The log ride

Which of course, I did

And the security guards arrested me

They couldn't find my Mom

So I had to sit there all day

In their little plastic

Mickey Mouse jail cell

They gave me a free Coke in the can though

The oppression began young for this crooner

+++

I need no great personality or even looks for that matter when it comes to her. In that brief second when she is in front of me, the playing field is leveled and all the cards are shown. She is not afraid to admit what most women are after anyways. My dollar bill is my access card to her. And the more I have of them the more she likes me. This is true capitalism at its finest I think.

+++

CNN said the following graphic pictures of dead Iraqi babies might upset some viewers. Fuck that! As soon as I saw those bombs going off and the subsequent blood stained ground and the baby's limbs lying on the hoods of cars, I just had to whip out my cock. Some people are shocked by shit like that. I'm a little different, that kind of shit makes me fucking hard.

+++

Oblivious we are

America

1776

How long will it last?

That's the question

250 years so far

But how much longer?

Egypt, Rome, Greece

Minoan, Ottoman, Mayan

Aztec, Byzantine, Persia

Incas, Celts, Vikings

All dominated the world at some point

But are now just Discover Channel

Specials on at 10 p.m.

Hordes of Narcissistic behavior

And world domination

Didn't stop their demise

It only

Hastened it

When an empire basks in all its glory

The walls and morals of their society

Crumble

I have seen America on this same path

For a while now

This destruction and collapse

From the past

Will be our future

Bush is no Caesar

Only little with extra sausage

Smart bombs, freedom fries, and Guantanamo Bay

Abu Ghraib, Folsom, the CIA

The suffering has just begun

My friends

This Act is not a Patriot

And neither are you

It's all going down around us

Blind to it

FEMA fucked up

Now the IRS wants to tax

Shit I put on eBay

"They" have been

Too wrapped up selling insurance

Meaningless

Real estate

Plastic goods

Chasing material items

HDTV

Buying that house

For security

Internet dating sites

2.5 kids are too many

Hitler loved BMWs

And so do you

Unfortunately for us

We will be the last to

Notice

Too busy watching the Oscars

Or some weak football game

Come back another time

Will you?

Oblivious, while basking in all our

Greatness

What greatness?

And celebrity worship

Plastic surgery horror stories

MTV plays only in hell

Cointelpro is not a new Timberlake song

There is no god above

That will save you

Grab a seat on a comfortable couch

Leather preferred

My friends

And watch it all self destruct

Combustible self

And crumble into nothingness

+++

My new policy towards women "Hole and a heartbeat" is working out pretty well for me. It's amazing how easy it is to get fucked around here when a person has no standards at all. No one ever pays attention to all those ugly fat chicks that are all around here. In my mind it's simple arithmetic really. The pond of beautiful skinny women is limited and there are massive amounts of more qualified candidates to fuck them other than me. But the pond of fat ugly women is enormous and let's be honest, they're just happy to get some cock, any cock really. They're easier to please and deal with as well. I put in no effort at all anymore. Hell, the other day I put my dick in a thing of vanilla Jell-O pudding snacks and got a fat girl to suck it off my cock. Now that's killing two birds with one stone right there.

+++

Everyone I went to Christian school with

Is dead or fucked up

Funny how that played itself out

Chris is doing eight years for meth possession

Matt, Jeff, and Steve are dead from the wheel

Mr. McCurry stuck his dick in the wrong

Parishioner's wife and got shot

Jessica has three illegitimate kids

We were the excluded and the shunned

The last lunchroom table

And seats at the back of the bus

Yet we all turned out halfway decent

I guess God didn't really like all those

Assholes very much after all

+++

My first day of Life Drawing class was last week. It was very odd walking in and setting up my paper on the easel and getting all my pencils out of my Ziploc bag knowing that in a few short minutes I was going to see a girl totally naked from 1:30 to 4:15 every Monday and Wednesday. And to think, some dudes actually pay to see this shit and here I am getting it totally for free for around five

fucking months; now that's fucking sweet! I had all my stuff set up and my
teacher went out to get the model. We were all discussing who it might be and
the consistent opinion was that we hoped for a large breasted blonde goddess
or something to that extent. After a few minutes, we heard the door knob being
turned. I watched as the door opened and my teacher appeared first and then a
guy followed behind her. "Who was this fucking guy" I asked myself? Maybe he
was the janitor or something? The teacher said "Class this is Tony. He's going
to be modeling nude for us the next few months." Where was my hot big
breasted goddess? Motherfucker! Of all the shitty luck and things to happen to
me in the world!

+++

A car with bright lights comes towards me

On a narrow road

Quiet suburban neighborhood

The same trashcans and mailboxes

Same color and same size

All painted black just like the song

Blood was in the air that night

Alcohol fueled and acceleration

Towards me

A Schwinn verses a Nissan Pathfinder

You don't have to be Einstein to figure out

Who would win this battle of physics

From right lane to left lane

He comes at me

Fuck!

He's trying to fucking run me over

To end my shit here and now

Fuck!

The Schwinn and the man on it go flying into

Several large green bushes

They brace the fall

But half his body eats dirt

You son of a bitch!

You motherfucker!

As he bleeds and extend one of his fingers

In the passing Nissans' general direction

That's all a loser can do

Hand gestures

And sit and bleed in a

Quite suburban neighborhood lawn

+++

Most people are absolutely clueless! That is a fact I truly know that's the truth. It seems to be getting worse though. Is it the fact that more ignorant people are breeding more than ever? I can't figure it out, but it sure seems that way. I think it starts at the top. Look at who our President is for Christ's sake. This is the best we have to offer here in America? This is the guy out of hundreds of millions of people that was best for the job? I don't think so. He actually is a perfect metaphor with what's wrong with America. He exemplifies that you don't have to be the best to get the job. It's no wonder jobs here are disappearing like a virgin on prom night. People are mindless drones these days. America truly is the place where mediocrity rules. I often wonder how we even became a world superpower. The mediocrity seems to be everywhere; from music, movies, politics, and news. Gone are the days when popular music was good music. There are no more people like Hank Williams, Buddy Holly, or Johnny Cash. Today we as a society worship mediocre rock bands and Britney Spears. We are obsessed with the ridiculous lives of mediocre actors and musicians. Our biggest selling magazines are People and Maxim which dumb you down, not inform and enlighten. I for one stand opposed to this dumbing down of people, New Zealand sounds good right about now.

+++

Does anyone else despise Valentine's Day or is it just me? I'm actually happy that I will be in my graphic design class tomorrow night until 9 p.m. so I don't have to hear about or be around any Valentine's Day bullshit. Don't forget to buy what you need for tomorrow tonight. There's nothing worse than standing in line for an hour at the grocery store to buy a gallon of milk while all those great fantastic people go for last minute candy and cards for that one person that "Supposedly" completes them. I don't know much I realize and I always have spent VD alone so maybe I'm just jaded, but if you don't appreciate your special someone the other 364 I doubt one day is really going to make up for that. I don't really need candy and card companies making me feel like a loser because I'm alone, Hallmark and Hershey's thank you, but I am alone and I'm ok with that. Shove your greeting cards and candy up your corporate asses!

+++

We see each other

But try and pretend like we don't

Fuck me!

I won't let her win

I can't let her win

I won't be the one to leave

She will be the one to leave

I come here all the time

Who the hell is she to invade my bar?

Fucking stupid bitch

She never wanted to come here with me

She said it was boring and

Nothing but a bunch of losers and assholes

Hung out in there

She was right about that

But what the fuck is she doing here?

Did she come here to rub it in my face?

Fuck me!

I'm very uncomfortable right now

I try and enjoy the conversation of my friends

More than I should

Just do it, pretend she's not there

She passes me on the way to the only bathroom

In the place

I tell myself not to look

But I do anyways

Like a car wreck I stop in my tracks and stare

She says nothing but she looks as well

She comes out of the bathroom

A few minutes later

In passing she says "Hi Brett"

I say "Hi" back

The truth and confrontation

Has once again

Been avoided

+++

My father was a brute of a person, inhumane and seemingly pissed off and bothered by my sole existence. I often wondered where his hatred of me came from. It made little sense to me as a child, but I'm probably even more confused now than I ever was then. From his appearance you would never guess what sort of a wretched human being he was. Maybe he was pissed off about being fat and bald, or maybe I was the reason he wasn't a swinging single anymore; I don't have the answers. I can still hear his voice in the back of my head to this day. His favorite little adjectives for describing me were "You little bastard," "Worthless bum," "Fucking loser," and his best line, the "I wish you were never born." The words for a while hurt worse than the violence, but after a while they still stung but you get used to it, I guess. He often came home from work around seven and before dinner would often find an excuse to chase me down and hit me for one of my supposed indiscretions as an eight-year-old. These offenses would often range from leaving my favorite G.I. Joe's like Snake-Eyes on the floor of the living room or for not coming promptly when called to wash up for dinner. He would often smell very odd to me. I didn't realize what Jack Daniel's was or what it could do to a person. I just knew it made his breath smell really bad and I always saw the bottle wrapped in brown paper on the kitchen counter. I often remember running and crying for my Mom to help me, to save me to take me away from this monster. I recollect putting a death grip lock on her feet as my father was pounding me with his fists and kicking me with his cowboy boots. She just stood there crying and was in as much terror as I was. His abuse of my mother as far as I know wasn't physical, but sure was pretty bad for her verbally. What could she do? What could I do? The only thing you can do sometimes is take it.

+++

John Mullinax was the greatest juvenile thief I have ever encountered. He was just known simply as Mullinax to those that knew him. No matter where you went, you wanted Mullinax there. You knew no matter if you had any money or not he would steal it for you if you asked him to. We started with candy, Cokes, and baseball cards originally, but as we became older we became bolder. Baseball cards and candy just didn't do it for us anymore. We upgraded to Walkmans, Nintendo games, and Les Paul guitars. I wasn't nearly as good as my friends Mullinax and Mark were. They could steal anything and they pretty much did. The balls and nerve they possessed as thieves was incredible to me.

+++

I told you that I loved you

But I didn't mean it

I will do anything for sex

This is a fact

Morals and values forgotten

Did they ever exist?

I said those words

Those lies

To gain your trust

If even for a second

And they expired

When the cum ran down

Your chin

+++

Me and Brian were sitting out on the patio of this bar the other day. We were enjoying ourselves until this fat bald redneck motherfucker sat down right next to Brian. Why do those guys always have to have the biggest fucking mouths on them? This guy was drunk and hitting on any girl that came into his cross-eyed range of sight. A group of twelve year old girls walked past us and I watched him clock them the whole time. As soon as they were past us a little bit, then came the "Hey baby, let me see some cooter." This guy was a class act for sure. Me and Brian sat there for over an hour in total shock as this redneck defiled women like I have rarely seen done before. The best of the night was when the guy hit on a barefoot pregnant girl that couldn't have been older than seventeen. His opening line was "Hey girl, come here and let me feel yer baby kick." He proceeded to try and run game on this pregnant chick for a few minutes. Everything he said disgusted me and made me want to clock him in the head, if for nothing else just being a complete moron. I felt bad for the barefoot pregnant girl until I saw the back of her shirt as she waddled away. It said "MILF" and something else after that which I couldn't read as my eyes were getting blurry from the booze. Since when can you be a "MILF" and only be pregnant? I guess she got what she deserved. Damn, sometimes I think only the people that shouldn't be fucking are and the people that should, like me, rarely or never do. God bless America!

+++

There's nothing worse then the Sunday after a three day orgy of alcohol. Having to deal with stupid humans at Kroger and the mall makes me want to kill. Most normal people have nothing better to do on Sunday than to get in my fucking way and get on my fucking nerves. I watched fat women in shorts jiggling their way into the potato chip aisle. I heard screaming kids while I waited in line. It could be a postcard, but Norman Rockwell never painted this. I try not to leave my shitty apartment on most Sundays, but this Sunday I had to.

+++

I saw you today. I walked towards you wanting to unload lyrical bullets of hate. I went to speak and instead of words, vomit came out. I went to speak again and even more greener vomit with small chunks of last night's pizza came out. I looked at you and gave you a weird little smile as vomit ran down my chin. That was the best goodbye I have ever given.

+++

Arranging a sexual encounter is like scheduling a doctor's appointment or ordering take out Chinese food really. I can see myself on the phone saying "Yea be here at ten and bring some booze with you baby if you don't mind. Thanks a lot, see you then, bye."

+++

Jenna Jameson rides on my antenna now

She's plastic and beautiful

And has a tattoo on her ass

I watch her twirl when I hit fifty

As the wind pushes her around and around

I like having a whore swinging on my antenna

I've seen her suck some really big dicks

And get double penetrated on VHS

Yet, there she is swinging on my antenna

She's my little plastic whore now

I wonder how long she will last

Until some fucking little shithead kid

Steals her from me

Then she will be swinging on someone else's

Antenna

That little dirty swinging plastic whore

+++

Ear plugs are the only way to go these days. Their lies aren't able to penetrate me that way. I just watch them now, dead silent. They look like little circus monkeys parading around and entertaining from a distance.

+++

I look past it and see ugliness of the leprosy kind

I smile when I really want to strangle

God forbid

Anything but a smile

That's all that matters, right?

A few muscle movements to let the humans

Know everything's great

+++

I was stumbling home drunk down Euclid Avenue at around four this morning. I was crossing the street near the park. The next thing I knew I was laying on the hood of a small silver car.

"Hey are you ok? I'm really sorry I didn't see you" As he tried to help me off the hood of his car.

"Yea man, I'm fine minus this glass in my hand."

"Get in and I'll take you to the hospital."

"Nah, don't worry about it man."

"Please just get in, you're bleeding badly."

"Nah, don't fucking worry about it man!"

"Here at least let me give you some money then."

After thinking about it for a second I said "Ok."

The guy reached into his wallet and pulled a wad of cash and stuck it in the front pocket of my jacket.

"I'm really sorry once again, you came out of nowhere."

"It's cool; just let me sit here for a while."

I woke up on the same sidewalk the next day. My first images were that of an older lady letting her dog take a shit near where I was sleeping.

+++

Suckered in by an unrealistic idea of happiness

Facade

Pain and hypocrisy were the hand I was dealt

By you

Anger, Rage, and Love

For you

The love is gone

Because of you

The hate remains constant

Because of you

My rage at every thought

Because of you

Burning mental pictures

Ending you

+++

I was dying for some food. I was drunk and hungry and there's nothing worse that that. I checked my wallet and all of my pockets and there was no cash anywhere. Fuck! I looked for change under the mat in my car and find almost a dollar in dimes, nickels, and pennies. I looked in my dashboard and found two dollars that I'd stuck in there at some point. The only place open that I could afford was McDonalds. The food is shitty but I guess I can't do anything about since I only have three bucks on me. The line at four in the morning was fucking endless. I smoked cigarettes and drank water as I inched my way up the line. Finally, after ten minutes I made it up to the speaker box. A fuzzy voice comes blaring out at me.

 "Can I take your order please?"

"Yea, can I get a double cheeseburger, a Coke, and a ninety-nine cent fry please?"

"Drive up to the 2nd window please."

"Ok."

A few more minutes passed before I finally made it up to the 2nd window. The very ugly fat white girl hiding under a blue hat asked me if I needed any sauce. I asked for ketchup and bbq sauce since they always only give you two packs of each one, which is never enough for the amount of food ordered. She handed me my drink and I put it in the cup holder in my car. She threw the sauce in the bag and extended it out to me. I had a grip on it, but where her fat hand had been left a nice little greasy hand imprint on the white crinkled bag. I pulled around near the playground and opened the bag. I stuffed my face with French fries. I noticed something odd in my mouth. I reached in and pulled out a large black hair covered in chewed up French fry. The site of it made me nauseous and I couldn't open my door quick enough before I vomited all over my lap. I removed the napkins from the bag and tried to clean myself up. There's only so much you can do with two small napkins really. I threw the bag out of the window and drove home hungry and drunk just as I had started out as.

+++

I went to a playground and ran with scissors because I believe in child safety

I walked into a Synagogue and saluted Hitler for exercise

I drank beer from a tampon to stop the bleeding

I stirred my lemonade with your dildo because I don't own a spoon

I fucked a Barbie doll in a Wal Mart bathroom because she was hot

I cursed a woman for being old because I'm a member of A.A.R.P.

I fondled a goat as a scientific experiment

I put my dick in the mashed potatoes before I quit out of angst

I punched a child because I was bigger than she was

I killed a clown for no reason at all

+++

I have a short Asian lady named Dr. Dong as my acupuncturist. I fucked-up again somewhere along the way and have another pinched nerve in my back. At least that was the diagnosis after little old Dr. Dong's evaluation of me. I had twenty-nine small gold needles stuck in my pale pimply hairy ass today to relieve the pain in my leg. I couldn't move. The needles froze my body. I tried moving my left leg after it started going numb, but a sharp pain hit me and I quickly changed my mind. Dr Dong hooked up what appeared to be some sort of jumper cables to the needles. She told me that they helped the needles penetrate deeper into my body or some shit like that. I felt sort of bad for the old man sitting with his shirt off at the table next to me. For thirty minutes this poor bastard had my pale pimply hairy ass staring right at him. No wonder every time when I looked over he had his eyes closed, and I can't say that I blame that poor bastard either.

+++

London's wrath

Bitter cold and soaking wet in the East End

My feet start to blister

Bland tea warms me

Bad food fills me

The Cure bore me

And the trains shake

The change from my pants

Oh my miserable London

You're no pinnacle of culture and history

No wonder my ancestors fled

You so long ago

+++

Me and John were sitting in Waffle House at five in the morning recently. And for no apparent reason we sat there in the fake wooden booth and concocted a plan to avoid paying for our breakfast. Even though we had the money to pay, I suppose the thrill of an illegal act just to see if we could get away with it was too tempting for us in our haze of alcohol. Our plan was for John to go and start his Honda two-seater and pull it up to the front of the Waffle House as soon as the haggard looking waitress brought us our tab to pay. Then, I would peruse the ticket as if I were calculating her arithmetic and tell her my friend felt sick and went to sit in the car. I would then proceed towards the front as if I were going to pay for the bill, then I had to run as fast as I could out of the two front doors and then hop in John's small Honda without us getting busted. Ok, let's go motherfucker!

+++

It's now twenty-one days until I will be twenty-seven years old. Fuck, I can't believe it. Just the other day I was nineteen. This shitty life is passing me fast. The quicker it's over the better off I will be. I've found all the truth I could here. Now it's time to find the real truth. The kind of supreme shit you can only know once you're dead.

+++

Parties thrown

But I wasn't invited

I was locked in my cage

From 9:16 p.m.

TNT roars on a cheap TV

Voices carry from downstairs

To my cage

A washcloth doused

In cold water

Brushes against my forehead

A fan is turned

To the "On" position

A door cracks

And a head protrudes

Only for a second

Twenty-eight of them were enough to know

My cage was better on this night

New Year's Eve Y2K

+++

A rotting tooth slowly begins its path towards final demise. Where once there were sanitary conditions and a glow of pearly white. Now there is only black and yellow staining and corruption to show the masses. When I smile, you run. I like the thought of that.

+++

I walked up to the Chevron earlier to get some beer. It's a ghetto gas station so there's not much of a selection of beer, there's mostly just malt liquor really. I grabbed a six pack of Budweiser and headed to the counter. I was halfway down the aisle when I saw two black guys run into the store and point their guns at the Indian cashier. I just froze and stood there watching, as did everyone else in the store. It looked like they were arguing for a second and the next thing I knew one of the guys shot the Indian cashier in the face. Blood splattered everywhere and I heard his body fall back into the cigarette rack and then on the floor. They grabbed what cash was in the register and ran out and hopped into a Honda Accord with tinted windows and sped off. I looked around and everyone had run out of the store. I grabbed another six pack of Budweiser and a bag of Doritos and ran out of the store myself. There was no need to get mixed up in that bullshit. I walked home with my six packs in hand and sat on the curb drinking away and replaying the crazy shit I had just witnessed in my head.

+++

Phone calls never returned

By me

Yet you keep calling

At least two times a day since we fucked

I wonder when the picture will become clear for you

How many more days will it take

I wonder

I admire your psychosis

In a weird sort of way

But I'm still not answering

You left a message asking me

If I thought I was too good to talk to you

No, I'm not

I'm just a fucking asshole baby

Sorry for that

+++

I was supposed to be outside my apartment at 7:30 p.m. I didn't get out there until 7:35 p.m. though. Where the fuck is Johnny at? We're going to be late to the Christmas party damn it. Hell, the only reason I'm going is to get some free food and my bonus check. The last thing I want to do is spend a Friday night hanging out with the fuckers I have to see every single day at work. I actually got semi-dressed up for this occasion. The party is down on Peachtree Street at some fancy pool hall/restaurant. Fucking John Ayers is a cheap bastard the other 364 days of the year so it was a pleasant surprise to see him splurge on having a party in an actual public place. I'm fucking freezing my ass off out here in the cold waiting for that son of a bitch to show up. I sat down on an old cross-tie in front of my apartment while I was waiting. The streets were empty and I could hear no sounds at all. It was the perfect night just to sit outside and enjoy the quiet sounds of the city that I have lived in my entire life. I lit up a cigarette while I waited. A few minutes later a guy passed me on the sidewalk and asked me if I had a smoke. I hesitated, but I gave him one of my Marlboro reds in the hard pack. No matter where you go in this town you can't escape these begging motherfuckers, even outside of my own damn apartment. Johnny pulled up a few minutes later; twenty minutes late as usual. Let's go get a drink on that cheap son of a bitch John Ayers. I'm going to drink until I puke tonight and John Ayers is paying for it all Goddamn it!

+++

I wake up covered in rats. They stare at me through non-existent holes in my walls. They laugh at me. They eat my food when I'm gone. They're unbearable. Their beady eyes peer towards my direction at all times. I punch holes in the walls trying to kill them. It's a futile effort. They scatter in every direction. I stomp on them as hard as I can but they never die or suffer injury. Over time I become accustomed to them. They are my only friends here late at night.

+++

I walked home drunk down Euclid Avenue as usual. I've walked that route more than I can remember. I know every crack in the sidewalk with a certain familiarity. I know where every trash can is and what every house looks like. My dungeon on Dixie Avenue is calling me. I don't want to go. It's miserable in there. There's nothing to do late at night but think. The air conditioner doesn't work and now that I'm home I'm sweating profusely. I have my bag of chips and that's about it. This life is killing me and shouldn't be lived this way.

+++

Indian store owners

Harassing bums as they

File past their store fronts

In mid-afternoon

Flies fuck and vomit

On rotten lettuce

Sitting in the corner

Of a filthy alley

Even dirtier hands

Meet cigarette butts

Left for dead on a clean sidewalk

Meals eaten in silence

And ants crawling on legs

Houses of cardboard

Demolished under economic viability

The Atlanta streets

Year 2001

+++

I admire your short white self. There are two blue stripes where the tobacco meets filter. The Marlboro logo is in an off black print. The L and the B look similar and run together at first glance. We met around ten years ago and we haven't left each other yet. I tried to once, but you came calling swiftly and replaced that horrible orange gum with ease. I grab a large BIC lighter and give you the burn you need to survive. I roll you between my fingers before taking my first suck. Glorious gray smoke fills my lungs and is released after a small delay. I admire your beauty with every movement towards my face. I watch the smoke fill the air after it's released from my lungs. I watch the red and orange glare and the sound, that unmistakable sound. Your burn runs towards my fingertips over time. If I'm not careful you leave me a permanent reminder of your power. Your life is short, usually four minutes at the most. Your death is ordained and smothered in circular blown glass. Don't fret my friend. Your singular death is accepted. But there are eighteen more of you left just in this pack alone.

+++

The liar within me

Once told a girl

That she took my virginity

Just so she would

Feel sorry

For me

And fuck me again

Fantastic pussy

Makes you do shit like that

Every now and then

+++

I hate my fucking job. Every day up at 6:15 in the morning and slave until almost five, and even sometimes later than that. Everyone I work with is broken and beaten. They all have bad marriages and fucked up kids. They work their asses off every day but have very little to show for it, as do I. I kill myself fifty hours a week to pay the rent on a shithole apartment with no hot water, air conditioning, washer and dryer, dishwasher, or any other modern convenience. The bathtub is about to fall through the floor and has turned a stale brown color. 794 Dixie Ave #8 Hell City USA. I get all the worst jobs at work since I've only been there a year and I'm the youngest. This is no great situation when you're a plumber. I get to go under crawlspaces covered with cockroaches, ants, snakes, and raw sewage. I get to vacuum up shit with a Shop Vac. I get to dig huge ditches in the sun. I get to stand in two inches of raw sewage. I get to lift heavy pieces of concrete. I get to shimmy into manholes of the city of Atlanta and become one with the entire population's waste products. This is no glorious lifestyle let me tell you. I make ten dollars an hour while my boss has a penthouse in Midtown. There is no future for me it seems. Something needs to change because I can't take this shit anymore. Hey, that was nice pun there.

+++

I got no money. I make almost minimum wage. Poor people just don't count, not now and probably not ever. It's a bleak future with very little options. This urban reality gives me no place to hide. I only get four hours of sleep a night. All my bills are late as usual. I hope they don't turn off my electricity. Maybe I can get some overtime this weekend. If not, I don't know what I'm going to do. Well I guess suicide is always an option.

+++

I'm sitting in the work van with Marvin next to some vacant mall at four in the morning. It's freezing outside. I smoke cigarettes and drink my coffee. Marvin snorts a line of speed to get him going. We should be inside working but the boss isn't here so fuck it and fuck him. I need a few more minutes to wake up and then it's back to the concrete. The concrete has been killing me the last three days. It's my job to take the saw and cut the concrete into huge blocks. Then I have to lug these chunks of concrete weighing near fifty pounds each up twenty-three steps and around the corner to the dumpster. My back is killing me and my hands are bleeding. I'm feeling forty instead of twenty-one.

+++

We went to a house today over on Moreland Avenue. The PVC pipes going down the backyard are stopped up and have been spewing shit water all over the basement of the house. Just my luck, it was my job to clean up this shit; no pun intended. I spent the first part of the first day throwing everything in the basement apartment away. Then the real fun started. I have a fifty gallon shop vacuum that I had to use to suck up the two inches of shit and piss that I was standing in on the floor. I almost threw up a few times. I had to wrap an old rag around my face just to deal with the smell. The vacuum sucked and sucked until the container was full of brown water. Unhook the top and lug that heavy fucker outside and to the backyard and empty, then roll the container back in and start over. I was covered in shit by the end of the day. There was really no way around that. Day number two wasn't much better, but I got it done and made my eighty-eight dollars. The shit I do for money!

+++

We sit there joking and smiling

Having a great time

At least I should be

But I'm dead inside

Alone and I know it

This emptiness no one can fill

Singular serving friends

On Friday and Saturday nights

Dead to me the other five days

Let's have another drink

Before anyone dares say it

The truth

+++

I'm sitting in a bar in Flagstaff, Arizona. It's cold outside. I'm in a bar I can't remember the name of. My friend's in the bathroom taking a piss. I order another pitcher of Budweiser while he's away. I make small talk with a cowboy sitting next to me. He says "Sure is cold out there ain't it?" I agree and say "Yea it is fucking cold out there partner." The cowboy asks me if I want to play a game of pool. I say "What the hell sure, but on one condition cowboy. I get to wear your big ass cowboy hat." The cowboy thinks to himself for a second and then gives me a little toothless smile. "What the hell, you seem like a good guy." The next thing I know I'm stumbling around drunk playing pool wearing another man's cowboy hat, truly feeling local in a little shithole Arizona town.

+++

It was my birthday today. No one showed up to hang out with me though. As always, it rained all day on my birthday. It's like a fucking hurricane out there right now. The bar is almost empty. There's just me and the bartender Joe as well as a few scattered drunks sitting alone at the booths in the back. I got up to go take a piss and wash my hands. When I came back I noticed a purse and a strange girl sitting at the stool right next to mine. She was gorgeous, way too gorgeous to be in this shithole on a night like this. I'm too nervous to say anything to her. I converse with the bartender Joe a little and she seems to pay to attention to what I was saying. She hears me say that it's my birthday.

"And just how old are you today?" she asks.

"Today I'm nineteen years old gorgeous."

"Let me buy you a shot since it's your birthday."

"Ok, Joe get us two Jager shots will ya?"

"My name's Brett by the way, what's yours?"

"It's nice to meet you Brett, you can call me Cindy."

We do a little cheer as our plastic cups meet. She says "Happy 19th Mr. Brett" as we down the Jagermeister.

She leans over and puts her hand on my shoulder and whispers in my ear

"Are you ready for your real present now?"

"What real present?" as I shrug.

She smiles at me and says "Come out to my car with me and you will find out, because I'm giving you the blowjob of the decade Mr. Brett."

"Check Please Joe!"

+++

The Laundromat I usually use is right across the street from this bar I go to. I always throw in my laundry and then go have some drinks. Everything was normal as always after the wash cycle was done. I stumbled back over to the Laundromat and put a stack of quarters into the dryer just in case I was drinking too much and was late to get my clothes. I sort of had it timed out by now since I'd been doing this every week after work for several years. Usually three Budweiser's in and my clothes would be dry. After three beers I stumbled back over to the Laundromat and grabbed a little cart and my large black garbage bag and headed over to my dryer. I rolled my cart up and my clothes weren't in there. The face of drunken confusion hit me. I walked around and looked in all of the dryers and no clothes looked like mine. I went and asked the Indian guy who is always in the dry cleaning part of the Laundromat if he had seen my clothes. He shook his head and said no. I went back into the Laundromat and once again looked in every dryer and this time every washer as well. They were nowhere to be found. This was too much to figure out when I was half drunk. I went outside the back door and lit up a cigarette as I plopped down in the crappy plastic chair out there. I needed some water so I walked to the gas station next door. As I approached the door I noticed this homeless guy who's always hanging around the neighborhood wearing my fucking blue Sick of it All sweatshirt. I yelled "Hey you motherfucker! Where did you get that shirt from?" He saw me and froze for a second, and then went running off towards the abandoned lot behind the store. I threw my cigarette down and went running after him. I couldn't run very fast since I had my work boots on, plus I was fucking drunk. I chased him several blocks down the street and then I lost him behind a house. I sat down on the sidewalk and lit another cigarette. Now I get to wear the same caulk and dirt soiled pants and shirt until I get paid next week.

+++

She towels my sweaty face and head after I'm done. I can't stop sweating though. She handed me the towel back after wiping my cum off of her chin. I wrap it around my waist and lower my head. My lips feel chapped and my hands are shaking. I breathe heavily as our eyes catch each other looking. Body odor and sex fills the air with their scents as I light a cigarette. I stare at the light it gives off as my mind goes blank.

+++

The silent darkness lasts forever now

From 5-8

The depression and angst builds

Slowly

The sun shines occasionally and I try not to notice

Glimpses of happiness are a farce

For the real shit happens from 5-8

Alone on the couch

Masturbating by my bed

Pizzas for one

Lit cigarette

And PBR in the can

Cold silent bike rides

TV companion set

And laundry to do

These are my friends from 5-8

My only friends from 5-8

+++

I got up at the usual time this afternoon, which was 2 p.m. I sat around in a towel for a few hours smoking cigarettes and watching TV with my feet plopped up on the kitchen table. I managed a shower by 5 p.m. and ran across the street to the pizza joint I eat at almost everyday and got my usual two slices and a sweet tea and took it back to the apartment. Three bites into my second slice my phone rang. It was "The work." "The work" calling me on my off day can't be good I thought to myself. The manager Jen was a little too nice to me over the phone so I knew immediately that she wanted something from me. Her words "Hey Brett I know it's your off day and all but Jerry didn't show up for work today is there any chance that you could come in and work for him?" Fucker! Since I really had nothing else to do I said sure as long as they would throw me some extra beers my way at the end of the night. Damn, I was covered in chicken guts and oil residue until five in the morning last night and now back on my off day, man this sucks. I slowly found my pants from last night in the corner hamper and put them back on. The smell of dead animals and particles of food still stuck on them. I put my black t-shirt on and slowly laced up my boots with the holes in the soles. One day I need to get a new pair maybe. I procrastinated for a few minutes more until I was at least fifteen minutes late and then I walked across the street to where I worked at. The manager thanked me for coming in and told the bartender to throw me a few extra beers at the end of the night and then she left, of course. I wondered why she couldn't stay and wash these fucking dishes herself. It was a pretty slow night overall. I just stood back in my little wash area and read the newspaper most of the night. I took way more breaks tonight then I usually do. I sat in a broken wooden chair outside the backdoor for a long time watching people

96

across the street drinking and eating and having an overall good time. I just sat there smoking cigarette after cigarette hating them from a distance. One of the local familiar homeless guys came up to me and asked me for some water. I got him a cup and gave him some water in it. I offered to fix him some food if he wanted it. He looked at me pretty surprised and said ok. I told him that I would be right back with some chicken fingers and fries. Ten minutes later I had him a big plate and handed it to him. It's always easy to be generous with the boss's money and I stick it to him whenever I can. Before too long the night was almost over. I pulled all the rubber mats out and washed them, and then lugged them back in again when we were closing up. Vick the bartender never gave me any extra drinks as I was promised. What a fucking surprise. My life is just a running never ending wasted night just to pay the rent and the electric bill.

+++

I don't like fucking beautiful women. There's too much of a chance that she will have some sort of vaginal power of persuasion over me. First, we're fucking, and the next thing I know, I'm over at her house watching some shitty Meg Ryan movie. That shit will never happen to me, thankfully. I like fucking mediocre, ugly, average, fat fucking whores. The sort of women that will fuck someone they meet randomly in a bar. Those are the women for me. I don't need someone to show off and impress my friends with. I just need somewhere to stick my dick for a few minutes every now and again.

+++

I'm done with it

I'm disconnecting the plug and tuning it out

The voices are screaming to be heard

My ego has been silenced

It's been a bad experience

A bad connection of wires soldered together from the start

The receipt was lost and they can't be returned

Newer and better parts were never discovered and used

The bottom fluid of a Bic lighter

Running on empty for thirty-two miles

Desperation on my face and me without answers

They will never come I foresee

+++

I went to take the trash out today that had been building up in my apartment. I tossed the three large bags filled mostly with clanging beer bottles and fast food in the large green dumpster. While I was out there I saw a white box lying near the dumpster so I walked over to check it out. I opened it up and bam; there was stack after stack of old porno magazines. It was like fucking Christmas in August! There was a little bit of everything at first glance. I saw copies of Playboy, Hustler, Club, and Juggs. I looked around to see if anyone was near. Once the coast was clear I lugged the near sixty pound box of porno magazines up the steep stairs of my apartment complex and up to apartment number 208. It looks like I won't be going out tonight.

+++

I knocked on your door today. You wouldn't answer the door but you spoke to me from inside. You said your roommate was sleeping and to come back later. I was hoping that you would answer the door naked, this didn't happen.

+++

My jaw is killing me. The stitches from where that asshole dentist cut my wisdom tooth out are hurting and pulling on my face. I can't open my mouth very well. Some people would be happy about that probably. There's definitely that girl that told me to get the fuck away from her the other night at the bar that I normally frequent. I don't even remember what I did to her, but I assume she didn't like it. I broke every rule the dentist said not to within several hours of my visit to his office. I drank, I smoked, and I ate pussy. Damn, I'm punk fucking rock!

+++

I wake up on the beach after a slight nap

There is a guy near me wearing a multicolored Speedo

He has a noticeable hard-on

But doesn't seem to notice or care

Everyone is pointing at him and laughing

I lay back down

+++

Number 53, that was me today. I don't even have a name in the doctor's office anymore, just a number and I sort of like it. I sat in the black massaging chair peacefully reading a book by John Fante. An old man, much like all old men kept telling life stories to this old lady with a heavy southern accent to my left. Stories of him farming in Connecticut and house prices in the grand strand area filled the room. Stories of past adventures from a lifetime away, part truth and part fiction, I'm sure as are the stories of most old men. It was hard concentrating on my John Fante novel with all the pointless conversation going on. The old lady with the Southern accent commented on how wood stoves are four times hotter than regular gas or electric heaters. And a "Black man" on her farm cuts the wood for her and her old decrepit husband. I guess just saying "A guy" on her farm was too educated for her simple old racist ass. She had to clarify that a "Black man" was laboring for her. The angst and anti social feelings hit me hard. Why did I leave my apartment? This is why I avoid areas where I have to associate with the public in any way shape or form. Finally, after page 121 the old man took his lies and damaged hand into the doctor's room. It was just me and the old lady now so maybe I could get some solid peaceful reading done now. That was until a slightly attractive blonde walked into the room and sat down right next to me, even though there were two open seats further down. Two pages into Fante and she began to fiddle with her phone, an obvious sign of boredom and not being able to handle public silence with strangers. First she appears to be texting someone, then I guess that wasn't enough, so she had to personally call someone.

"Hey baby."

"Look we need to get the BMW looked at before we go to Maryland."

"Yea, my mom has the Volvo, maybe we can use hers."

"What do you want for dinner?"

"Well maybe I can pick something up."

"No, he didn't."

"I can't believe that."

"I just had a baby so I can't."

"Well maybe I can help relax you later tonight."

I shit you not, this is what I had to listen to for around twenty minutes, right fucking next to me the entire time. I finally sat Mr. Fante down on the table and just gave her a look like I wanted to stab her. She saw me and my fury and took the conversation outside of the room. I swear, when will people get over the fact that the world does not solely exist or revolve around them. It always amazes me that people are such egomaniacs. A few short minutes later number 53 is called. See you later you rude cunt.

+++

Dead animal carcass on the White House lawn

Serial killers knitting a new quilt with my Grandma

Puppets on the hands of abused children

Weathered faces protruding giant Botox nails

Thirteen staples in my celebrity eye

Skateboards and dirt roads say dead end

A shiny new rock in my hand

Self mutilation with a plastic spoon

An Astronaut pen to write on a rock

Vomit spewing from

Hairy armpits and Kool-Aid are instant gratification

+++

I got home drunk and scavenged the fridge and every drawer in the house for something to eat. In the back of one of the drawers I found an old pack of shrimp flavored Ramen noodles that I guess one of my roommates had left here sometime ago. The water had been turned off for a while now, and so had the electricity for that matter. I found a half bottle of Budweiser that I'd left in the fridge a few days ago to go with my new found noodles. I opened the pack of noodles and put them into a large white plastic bowl. I shook the seasoning packet into the bowl as well and then added a little Bud to soften them up. I picked up the little square blob of noodles and seasoning and Budweiser and bit into it as hard as I could. I felt a crack instantly. I opened my mouth and pulled out one of my front teeth. I looked at it for a second and then popped it back in my mouth and then swallowed it. The tooth fairy stopped coming to my house a long time ago so why not right? I picked up my Ramen noodle blob again and took a smaller bite this time and then I felt another crack. This time, it was one of my bottom front teeth. I reached into my mouth and pulled it out with ease. I took it out and examined it. This one had a small brown spot on it. I guess it was a cavity. I popped it back into my mouth and swallowed it as well. I got about halfway through the blob until I heard another crack and again it was one of my front teeth. This time it was stuck in the blob of Ramen noodles. I pried it from the blob and again swallowed it down with ease. Everything is a blur after that. I guess I had passed out from all the booze I had consumed earlier in the evening. The next thing I remember was waking up the next morning wearing the same clothes from the night before and sleeping in a pool of blood coming from my mouth. My eyes were all swollen and I stumbled into the bathroom to take a piss. After I was done, I looked in the mirror and I counted seven teeth missing. I wasn't hungry anymore so I guess it was worth it. I went to Kroger later in the day and bought some of those fake plastic Dracula fangs they sell in the quarter machines near the exit. I'm looking good as new now.

+++

I chanced my luck and hauled ass through a Colorado snow storm. I drove until my head hurt and my eyes were about to pop out of my head. I got a cheap hotel room at Motel 6. After warming up a little I walked down the street to a Denny's. I sat alone as I ate my Grand Slam Breakfast. The eggs were cold and tea wasn't very sweet, but who gives a shit, I'm a fucking road warrior! I paid my bill and went for a walk in an unknown Colorado town. I was the only person around for miles and it was great.

+++

Annoying bird on my window

A giant turd swimming in my pool

It smiles at me as I walk by

I smile back

BB gun resting on my shoulder

That bird is gonna die

I'm surrounded by classy people

Covered with peanuts

One shot

I missed

Reload

Swimming pants on

Playing with my friend

Marco Polo rings out loud

There is no response

Thump on the ground

Wings flapping

As brains cover the ground

Brown splash

My friend disappears into a million little pieces

I will have a bigger and better one later after that Chinese buffet

+++

PBR makes me a "Fuck god." No Viagra or Spanish Fly needed here ladies. Just let me down enough of my love drug in the red, white, and blue bottle until I can barely stand; and then you will find out its mystical powers of love. It also helps that my little secret turns fat girls skinny and makes wretched women seem saintly. Here's to you my best friend, available in both the bottle and the can.

+++

Young yuppies are all around me

Cruising the streets

In foreign luxury cars

Beautiful blonde hair seated next to you

Blowing in the wind

Only there until you bleed

Wearing their large bank accounts

Like a noose around their necks

Keep grinding away

In that cubicle

To make the payments

Kissing ass

Taking names

The devil's handshake

Lust and ambition

Is a sign of weakness

Be nothing and a no one

Why try at all?

We all end up ten feet underground

In the end

Covered in maggots

And the rotting smell

Of once human flesh

+++

Please forgive me God. I've lost track somewhere since all my Christian schooling in my younger years. I'm sitting on the front porch now, smoking one of my last three cigarettes and drinking a Budweiser that I found hidden under some apples and water bottles in the bottom of my refrigerator. There's blood covering my boots now. I washed my hands after I did it, but I gave up on getting the rest off of me. My wife and two children are sitting peacefully on the couch now. In fact, it's the first peace I've had in ages. There was no need turning on the television for them since they're all dead anyways. I put my favorite Hank Williams album on the turntable instead. It's been years since I was allowed to listen to it in peace. "I'm So Lonesome I Could Cry" still sounds better on vinyl than it ever will on CD. I don't know what to do now. Do I make a run for it with no money or do I call the fucking pigs and turn myself in? It's a paradox really. "Fuck it," I'm going to the gas station down the street for another six pack and then I'll decide.

+++

I was working in the porn store as usual that day. It was a pretty lame job. I had my elbows on the counter watching Sanford and Son reruns trying to pass the time as usual. There was an obviously married man browsing the gay porn DVD section and two drag queens looking at the realistic Jenna Jameson latex vaginas, as well as a very butch looking lesbian browsing the dildo aisle. A man dressed like Burt Reynolds's character from "Smokey and the Bandit" walks in the door and it shuts hard behind him. The bells attached to the door crash against the door frame. It was a flash of denim from aisle to aisle. His cowboy hat gave away his location when I couldn't see anything else. The "Mustached one" brought his selection of three videos and placed them on the counter. They were all part of a "Barely Legal" series. He handed me a one-hundred dollar bill and said "Hey man you gotta-get-em while they're young partner." I just looked at him with an awkward smile on my face as I counted his change out to him. I put his videos in a non-descript black bag and handed them to him. Only three and a half hours to go and I'm out of this dump for today.

+++

The world ended today but we were the last to know

We finally got what we wanted

The humans have returned to captivity

Our leashes bound by a confused society have been lifted

We truly can run free now

Just me and you

+++

It seems that I'm the one person evolving on this planet. I'm happy to get older. I'm falling apart a little bit every day. New scars appear where there were none before. Cuts on my hand from building shit and scabs on my face from shaving are giving me more and more character each and everyday. I don't want to die pretty. I want to die ugly, eyes open, and alone. We are all rotting flesh anyways so what difference does it make anyways. People that get plastic surgery are trivial and vain to me. Fuck your self esteem and weak mind! Most of the time what's wrong with you is in your head not your body. A pair of fake tits doesn't make you more attractive, it shows the lack of guts and inept brain you're carrying around. You were brainwashed somewhere into believing a lie. Maybe you watched too much TV or let the kids at school get to you, who knows? All I know is that if someone dug me up I wouldn't there to be a pile of bones and two bags of silicone resting on my chest; but that's just me. You people can run out and try make yourself look better if you want, but I will be here bearing the wounds of a life lived. I want to push my body to the extreme and leave it wounded and bearing my mark.

+++

I wish women were as easy to deal with and innocent as they seem in most Ramone's songs. There's a childish brilliance in their lyrics that I appreciate. Just listen to "I Wanna Be Your Boyfriend" or "Rock and Roll High School" and you will see what I mean.

+++

I cut my chin badly while shaving today. It would probably help if I didn't use razors until they're full of hair and turn into cheese graters. The blood spewed everywhere and wouldn't stop. I just sat in a chair and watched it drip onto my towel. I didn't try and stop it. I licked some off of my chin. It wasn't bad I must admit. I now bathe daily with that same white blood stained towel.

+++

Toe nail clippings

Of the gods

Toilet bowl of shit

Sits covered with vultures

Developing sores in Ghana

The care package sent C.O.D

Dead babies dancing at their ten year

High school reunion

Dying leaves of Burnt Sinai

Rest on my broken windshield

Begging forgiveness

For all the cruelty caused

But no forgiveness will be given this time

A soon to be mother screams as she

Inserts the coat hanger into her vagina

And turns

One last time

+++

It won't be long before I'm gone from this place. I'm tired of it and I've been bored with it since I got here. The people are bullshit and predictable. They are lame to the point that they don't even realize it. Basically, I can explain it like this, they are one step above rednecks who think trendy fashion comes from a generic store in a mall and a great time is dancing in tourist trap nightclubs drinking overpriced beer. That is not exactly my scene or any type of human being I would want to know. There are very few I will stay in touch with when I'm gone. I have very few things keeping me here. I just would like to finish one fucking thing in my entire life. I knew it was going to be hell, but I will persevere. I will make it because I'm a grunt and I can take anything. I just hope some of me survives. I feel all alone here. It's tough but I survive. This is the first time I've ever lived anywhere that I didn't have a friend I've known for ten years beside me. Maybe all I need is a sidekick and everything would be fine. Batman had Robin and Brett will have (insert random name).

+++

Women

I hate you all

You dirty bitches

You whores

Use your tits

And asses

To get whatever you can

Out of someone

I know your game

Your neurosis

Head games and fake emotions

I'm wise to it

I rarely say anything about it though

I don't want you to know that I know

Your game

When I make you cry and feel

Like a slut

I smile

+++

You say I'm real, yea I'm just like you, sometimes. I breathe polluted air and urinate most times in a toilet. I drink too much, I pay bills, and I drive a car, is that real enough? I'm as American as you could get. I come from an abusive background, and no, I didn't get enough hugs as a child. I went to cookouts and played baseball. I hated my family and did drugs to piss them off. I fuck up a lot. I try and learn from mistakes. I'm ugly and jaded and probably mentally disturbed in a lot of ways, is that real enough? I'm alone and crave affection on occasion. I often don't like what I see in the mirror. I wish my life was different and much better than it really is. I'm hateful, petty, jealous, vindictive, temporal, bitter, happy, sad, inept, goofy, embarrassed, lazy, shallow, racist, pathetic, liar, smart, rejected, exiled, greedy, envious, sexist, passive, boring, rigid, shrewd, and curt, the same as you are at times.

+++

A concubine of

Liars and hypocrites

Smiles on the outside

Demonic brutality

Awaiting me on the inside

A handshake extended

While holding a knife

In the other

Forgive me for trusting

Friends

Until the end

+++

It's funny sometimes how easy life can make a total u-turn on you. I'm often curious about how one act can change a life so easily. I went and bought a gun today from Dick's pawn shop. It's a beautiful 9 millimeter. It's solid black which fits me fine. The edges are smooth and it's easy to conceal in my combat pants. I'm jealous of God; he can kill at random and pay no consequences for it. I want to be like him, the greatest serial killer in the history of the world. People often refer to it as "God's will." How great is that? I want to kill. To see what it's like, to see if I have the guts to do it. I want that power and feeling of a deity. Just like God, I will choose my victims at random. The first person with a smile that I see gets a 9 millimeter bullet in the face. Will people refer to it as "Brett's will?" I doubt that very much.

+++

Skateboarding on Waddell Street

Patches of smooth pavement

Beneath me

Give way to rocky terrain

Cracks in the sidewalk

Rocks

Branches

Deter my movement

Same houses as always

Same day care center

Homeless man walking

Talking to no one

I sit and watch

Large hill

I muster the nerve to do it

The sun is setting in the East

No cars coming

Fucking go man

Wind blowing in my face

A patch of sand and rock that I didn't see

Crash

Teeth lying on pavement

Bloody arms and legs

Knees and hands

Spitting blood by the gallons

Limp back to the small apartment

Picking rocks out of my skin

Hydrogen Peroxide

I love that smell

+++

I walked past you and I didn't recognize you. You had changed form. You were no longer beautiful and intoxicating. You were hideous and repulsive. Your body had inverted itself somehow. Your soul had taken form. Your features now reflected the soulless generic qualities you possessed. Your liver and spleen were beautiful and intoxicating now. But one cannot love a body part unfortunately. I walked away from you as you started to speak and never looked back.

+++

I called you from jail. I called everyone I knew actually, but no one answered. That's the way it always is, no one is ever around when you actually need them. When the shit hits the fan you're always left alone. That's the way most people work, especially all those "Good" friends that you or I have. In the end, when they are needed, they are nowhere to be found. Since I'm allowed to keep calling someone until I talk to them, I said the hell with it and dialed 1-976-Hot-Pussy instead. At least I know where I stand with those bitches. Number 06271979 is being called on the overhead speakers, it's back to cell #321 for now. I'll be talking to my new and only friend "Star" again real soon. You can count on that.

+++

I met this girl in a bar tonight. I was so drunk I can hardly remember anything about her. I guess that means that she was neither particularly beautiful nor particularly ugly. Mediocrity is a good thing on occasion I suppose. She bought me something to eat at the bar we were drinking at. It was a chicken sandwich with only ketchup and cheddar cheese on it with a side of fries. As I went to bite into the sandwich, the piece of chicken fell on the floor. That sucked because I was starving. I ate a ketchup bun instead and walked home drunk and alone as usual.

+++

Fat girl muff, it must be horrible going down on them. I can imagine their disgusting bearded husbands covered in dirt from the labor job they work all day just licking away on her big fat pussy. Her stomach rolls bunch up as she spreads those fat jiggly legs for him. I wonder how he gets it up for her. I bet the smell is nauseating. There's no way that bitch could clean that fat muff very well. The shit he must imagine while fucking that cow, now that would be something to find out. He probably thinks about their daughter in the next room or her skinny better looking sister, I know I would. No thought would be too fucked up. In fact, that guy should be given a medal or a tax break for doing that act.

+++

People I know always assume that other people like myself want to hear about their pointless lives. Yea, please waste my time and life telling me about who you're fucking or what happened at your trivial job the week before. If I wanted that from a friendship I would watch that stupid show Friends on TV.

+++

Concrete lays way to a bleak landscape

Greed and gluttony, oh my capitalist beast

Corporate isolation

Surrounding me

Covering me

Smothering me

With their trademarked logos

Of hate and oppression

Atom bombs are released in euphoria

As the suburbs of utopia lay in rubble

White men turn to charcoal colored dust

The lab rats are released from captivity

They sit on my couch and watch TV

Growing disillusioned and obese

They truly are Americans now

Value sized and cheap

+++

My best pickup line of the week was this "I like your new haircut. It makes me want to put it in your ass even more now." Said to a girl I know that works at the usual bar I get drunk and stumble around in.

+++

Chase the money. That's what you have been pre-programmed to do from the start. Sell what little dignity and morals you have for it, that's the real American way and dream isn't it? I want no part of that bullshit. I would rather be destitute the rest of my days. It's all I know anyways. I'll sit back and watch though. Your goals and dreams of home ownership are a farce to me. Everything you own in the end owns and controls you. Keep paying those bills and building good credit history. You deserve to be a number on a computer program just like all the others out there.

+++

I haven't fucked in a while. Man, I need to though. I can feel the cum in my balls backing up and dying to be released. I jerk off but it does little good, it only delays the inevitable act that needs to be undertaken. So much effort it takes these days to get laid. I don't know if I have it in me right now. Where are the sluts I can just mumble a few words to and go straight to the act of fucking at? I just need the act. I don't need any cuddling or hanging out afterwards, just the fuck ma'am, just the fuck.

+++

How many fingers can I get inside of you? I tried one and it worked. I tried two and it worked. I even tried three and it fit also. I got bold and tried four. Five was up next and miraculously that fit as well. My hand was next, a bold move I know, but that fit as well. I pushed all the way up until I was elbow deep in wet pussy. I grabbed your eggs and ripped them out and laughed like a weasel while I held them in my hand. I was like Napoleon conquering Egypt. Victory was at hand, no pun intended. Whores like that shouldn't be allowed to poison the world with their seed. I made sure that wouldn't happen.

+++

Lust like rats

Caged and grotesque

Skirting and breeding

In the sewers of life

Underground and rarely seen

Poking its beady little eyes

Out from the depths

The depths of despair

It's a feeling I know well

And so do you my friend

+++

Sickness has stricken me. I don't know what the fuck I've got but I'm on my fucking death bed. My head is spinning and I don't know what the fuck is going on. I go into the bathroom and peer into my mouth. My tongue is covered in a thick white coating. I down pill after pill but I don't feel any better. I sleep for eleven or twelve hours and it does no good, and makes me even more tired than I already was. I went to the doctor. I made light conversation with the nurse. She takes my blood pressure and temperature. I get led into a white room with bad lighting and told to sit on a non-descript white table. The doctor comes in, I tell her my symptoms and she says ok. She gives me free medicine and I go home. I don't feel any better after another week. I go back to the doctor after being on my death bed. Same as before, I make conversation and get my stupid blood pressure taken again. The doctor finally agrees to give me some fucking real medicine for once, thanks. I pay my twenty bucks and stand in line with all the other senior citizens waiting on their prescription drugs to get filled. I down four white pills when I get home, maybe now I'm on the road to recovery.

+++

Perfection is something you can't achieve

Nice teeth

Great skin

And a perfect body

Mean nothing

When you're a carcass

That's the only time when human beings

Are beautiful at all to me

The only time we're all on a level playing field

Is when we're all fucking dead

Ha Ha Ha

+++

We walked out of Masters with a stripper my friend knew. Boom, we get to her plastic Japanese car, and of course, she doesn't have her keys. Only a stripper has these problems. She suddenly remembers and remarks about how her boyfriend has the keys. She calls him and I overhear him say "I'll be there in ten minutes." We end up of course waiting for an eternity. Phone call after phone call never answered or returned by this mysterious boyfriend. We freeze our asses off because of this prick. I start making out with my lady friend in the

Master's parking lot. That made the wait less painful. I remember my trusty Bad Religion jacket that I had in the backseat of my Jeep. I go and get it and put it on. I don't offer it to either of them because I'm a selfish prick basically. I'm from Georgia, and I can't take the fucking cold goddamn it! We wait for almost an hour and I say "Fuck this guy, let's go get a drink at Ron Jon's." Both girls agreed, so I drive the stripper and my lady friend over to the bar. I get a drink and stand by myself. The girls talk about whatever, I don't know actually. Then the stripper proceeds over to me and says "Hey can I borrow your car to go get my boyfriend," which I reply "Are you fucking kidding me? I don't even know who you are." And besides, that prick is the reason I froze my ass off for an hour. The stripper looks bummed out that I won't loan a total fucked up stranger my car. She eventually suckers or begs a ride off someone else to go and get her shithead boyfriend who was drunk at another strip club down the street. This incident just further strengthens my statements that people that work at strip clubs are the most fucked up people on the planet, period.

+++

Eyes burning

My poison invades the late night air

Lemonade stands of deceit being sold

By the glass

Pretty blonde haired angel of lust but

A devil in sheep's clothing underneath

Twenty-five cents a lie

Being sold and bought

Be weary of who you trust

My friend

That pretty blonde haired angel of lust eventually

Turns to dust

+++

Nine months developed

Circumcised and breast fed

Dress me up and parade me around

Crucified like Jesus I'm even

Trained to take a dump

Crying and teething a pat on the back

Respect your parents

Try and be good and

Reflect their values and morals

Don't embarrass them in public

Toys of color and strollers filled with puke but

Don't eat the glue

Shit stained diapers and thrown diced food

Lied to and abused from the very start

+++

I wish for death on a daily basis. Most people wake up everyday the same as everyday before and carry on with the normal doldrums of a normal everyday life. I wake up most of the time hung over and sounding like Darth Vader after the mass amounts of cigarette smoke inhaled from the previous evening. I scratch my balls and take a piss. I say to myself "Today is as good a day to die as any" and then carry on my normal routines of everyday life. But as I'll be driving around I'll pray that car slams into me and takes me out, or I think about flooring it and ramming the car ahead of me. My only fear is that I wouldn't be taken out. It would be my luck that I would just be really fucked up and paralyzed only to live the rest of my days in constant agony. Eating the gun is the only sure way in my mind.

+++

There I sit a world away. Bored and hating the world at 3 a.m. Suicide always makes sense late at night for some reason. Doing it during the day just doesn't have that element of coolness to it. If you're going to off yourself, I would assume it's better to hang yourself in the late night hours when the depression is at its best, and then be found the next afternoon when your overweight roommate comes home from work and finds you dangling from the living room ceiling fan.

+++

I drown myself in booze almost everyday. The only pleasure I know. The only regrets I have are the next day. The hangovers add up like simple arithmetic. Pretty soon they aren't even hangovers anymore but everyday life. Who's to say the differ really? One man's paradise is another man's version of hell.

+++

I used to be a nice guy before I got here. But after three years in this shithole, the place has sucked it out of me. Now I don't care. For the most part people are so fucking stupid here that I really can't help but treat them like shit and laugh at their idiocy. I find myself more cynical and jaded than ever before now. This is what happens when Brett's life lacks a lot of fun on a regular basis. Fun doesn't exist here. It sounds lame I know, but I would rather be alone than hang out with ninety percent of the people I know in this town. I don't know if this is a good thing or a horrible thing that I have become. Was I blind and trying to live in a happy world that didn't exist before? Or, have my eyes been opened to just how stupid and predictable people are? Or, are there just more per capita of idiotic generic human beings here than anywhere I have been before? They don't seem that way when I leave here. I don't know. I'll figure it out before I finally get the fuck out of here one day soon.

+++

Latex gloves survey my mouth. Giant needles are poked into my flesh several times and an unknown substance is pushed into these tiny pricks. Numbness follows as I try and relax and take it. Jokes are spoken but I can't laugh. Their devices of torture are clamped and screwed into me. Drills of pain and valor are used as their prodding tools. Water flows and the taste of blood fills my throat. Sucking devices rid me of what soul I have left. Needles of various sizes are poked into me for an eternity of time. After an hour or two I rise. Jokes are told and I laugh now. I shake hands with this demonic doctor of pain. I pay their toll and proceed into the afternoon sun.

+++

Love is for them

I know better

I know not to let them in

Never trust them

And never believe any of their beautiful lies

That protrudes from their soft lips

Selfish intentions and money

Are what they're after in the end

That's what we're all after

In the end

Selfish intentions

A cure for loneliness and isolation

There is none

For that disease

Women only make the situation worse

+++

I came home as usual from my nine hours of construction work. It was around 5:30 p.m. when I got home. I lugged my toolbox up the all too familiar stairs. The home and the wife were my yoke. I dreaded what was coming as soon as I opened the door. Like clockwork "Hey hun, how was your day?" Hearing those words took a little life out of me everyday.

+++

Mother's day?

I have no mother

I'm a bastard child of a

Disturbed society

Gone mad

A trashcan baby found by wolves

And raised in the wilds of an urban landscape

+++

We were driving back from the bar in your slightly rusted green Oldsmobile. I have bad feelings sometimes but usually nothing happens. This night was different though. We were about to turn onto my street when I saw the blue and red lights flashing. My first thought was "Fuck." I tried to compose myself. I put on my seatbelt, which I never usually wear. I drank what was left of my orange Gatorade and then lit a cigarette as the cop approached the car. "License and registration please" were the first words out of the cop's mouth. I fumbled around in the dashboard until I finally found it hiding under packs of matches and several lighters. I handed my registration and license to the cop. He looked them over and then he asked me if I'd been drinking. I responded with the usual "I had a few drinks with dinner" response. He then asked me what my girlfriend had been drinking. I said she was trashed and I was her "Designated driver." He said that he had to run a check on my plates and then he would be back. I said "Could you make it quick because this bitch gives the best drunken blowjobs I've ever had in my life."

The cop looked at me and then said "No shit?"

I said "Yea trust me partner."

"Well I can tell you're obviously drunk as hell sir, but I might be willing to look the other way this time."

"Ashley get out of the car and go with the cop."

"But why Brett, what are you up to?"

"Just go with him baby."

She got out of the car and stumbled towards the white police car. I started the engine back up as she opened the door. My last memory of Ashley was seeing her head bobbing up and down near the steering wheel of the cop car as I swerved back onto the road. I'll be home in a few minutes just in time to catch reruns of the Golden Girls.

+++

I wish that I was as

Cool

As you are

You're bringing sexy

Back

You have tons of friends

I don't

Your beauty intoxicates men

And makes women jealous

Craving plastic surgery

Just to one up

Your genetic predisposition

Your brain is never used

For practical or important

Purposes

Only to decide which dance club

To "Hit up" on Friday Night

Or which color of

Prada purse goes with your

Shoes

I feel sad for you in a way

A whole life wasted

On mediocrity

Music, movies, hobbies

Life in general

Why exercise your brain

When men only want your cunt

In the first place

I hate to be the bearer of bad news

But

Men only talk to you

Buy you drinks

Are nice to you

Because of that sweet cunt

And pretty face

Which is fading with age

In time

You will be cast aside

For the newer

Younger

Better looking

Girl

With bigger tits

And a smaller brain

How ironic life cycles are

Holla dumbass

+++

"You know I'm sick of seeing that bitch in here."

"Which one?" Sam asks.

"That bitch over there by the dart board in the black top."

As the man's head jerks to his left

"Oh yeah, she's in here all the time isn't she?"

"Yea she is and I'm sick of goddamn seeing her fat face!"

"Yea, I know what you mean."

"Seriously, I feel like going over there and kicking her right in her fat pussy."

"Ha-ha, man you have serious problems."

"It's a possibility man."

"I don't really give a fuck anymore you know."

"At least it would be something different."

The small waitress with blonde hair passes the table and the conversation halts. She passes with a large pitcher of beer and the conversation continues.

"I'm just sick of this shit around here you know?"

"I'm not asking for much, hell just seeing a new face walk through that door would be enough for me right now."

As the man points his index finger towards the large wooden front door of the dark tavern

"I need some fun for fuck's sake."

"My life might as well be one never ending theatrical play of déjà vu."

"Who knows, maybe I'm just sick of life in itself."

"And then again, maybe I just need some fucking pussy."

Sam laughs as a smile creeps up on the other man's face

"Yea that couldn't hurt."

"Hell, I'm even sick of jerking off, that's how bad it has gotten."

"Jesus, I don't want to hear about that shit man."

"Sorry man, how about another beer?"

"Alright, I'm going to take a piss."

+++

The parking lot of lunacy was my second home. It sounds very odd and void of a soul doesn't it? It was a huge square of blacktop with yellow stripes here and there marking the designated parking areas for shoppers and drinkers. A lot of my free time was spent in this one particular parking lot. I don't really know or understand why now that I revisit it in my mind. Maybe it was a cheap way to drink and hang out with friends I guess. A majority of them I didn't really even care for or relate to in any sort of humanistic way. It was like being the photographer in Vietnam or the journalist on the front lines of occupied France in WWII. I was there for the spectacle and the insanity. That's the only reason I can come up with anyways. Every weekend I would be there drinking it seems like. Sometimes we would play music and sometimes we wouldn't. The idea was to just stand around drinking and telling each other who we were fucking or who we wanted to fuck and the occasional raunchy joke was thrown in for good measure. On one particular evening, there were perhaps fifteen of us fucking around in the parking lot as usual. Homeless people were everywhere in the neighborhood so I was used to them asking for change and hassling me on my way to the bank or gas station. But this one guy made the mistake of asking one of the insane dudes that was hanging out down there for change. A few of the guys were fucking with him and asking him why he smelled so bad and shit like that. The next thing I knew, one guy just clocked him in the face. The homeless guy didn't go down, but he stumbled back a few steps. Then another guy punched him in the head and he went down hard. A few people ran over in the insanity of the moment and started kicking him and yelling at the guy. He just curled up in the fetal position and tried to avoid the onslaught. Me and the three girls there were in shock. We kept asking each other what the fuck was going on and why the hell were they doing this to a homeless guy. One of the guys thought it would be funny if they threw him in a large green dumpster in the back of the parking lot. Four of them grabbed his arms and legs and proceeded to throw him in the dumpster. No one really said anything after that. It was the calm after the storm. A few seconds later we heard sirens and everyone started clearing out. I was glad someone called an ambulance. On my way out of the parking lot I ran over to the dumpster and took a quick picture of the destruction. The guy was bleeding pretty badly but he was still alive which I was grateful for. I walked off as well and headed to the nearest bar across the street for a drink. I told you those days were crazy.

+++

I was registered in school

But that didn't mean I ever went

The truant officer came by the house today

While I was skateboarding and at the local library

A few days later

I usually checked the mail

But I had forgotten this once

And my father found the letter

From school that said I hadn't been there in

Almost two weeks

As I did always

Getting up early and pretending I was headed

To school

Watching TV and eating cereal on the floor

A swift hard unknown kick to the ribs

By good old father

Was my penance for this

I got up and took a shower

Stole a few bucks out of his pants

To provide the days cigarettes

And went to the library as always

And read Medical Journals all day looking for

Any pictures of naked girls or tits

That I could get my hands on

+++

Oh, what a rush it is to put that folded rag paper dollar bill in a stripper's garter belt. I can feel my hand rub her smooth thigh as the money slides right in next to the other assortment of denominations. For a brief second we are alone and in our own little universe. Her fake tits brush against my face and her perfume intoxicates me. Her hands grab my shoulders as she lunges my head into her breasts. I smell them and I can feel them, but I dare not taste them. And then suddenly she is gone. Another dollar bill shakes from an extended hand a few chairs down.

+++

Solitary confinement is the only present I want

That I need

Wrapped neatly under fake plastic trees

The front door under lock and key

Tempt me and ruin this dream deferred

I must on occasion deal with these mongrels

Growing more ignorant and annoying

Every second

Every hour

Every year

Every decade

And every century

They're fucking animals out there

Without conscience and lack of any remote

Chance of decency

They will brawl each other in large lifeless dim lit stores

Over a new video game console

Or a fucking red talking doll

All while waving the old red, white, and blue

While they go further into corporate debt for cheap sweatshop

Chinese and Singapore imported goods

I don't think this is what Locke, Franklin, or Nietzsche

Had in mind

You can't deal with mediocre organic matter like them

One can only tolerate and shake a head in disgust

At what they have become

+++

Today I was determined to get some painting done for once. In my mind, I thought that by 9 p.m. I would be hard at work and covered in oils. I was still drinking coffee and smoking cigarettes at 10:37 p.m. I said to myself, after I take a shit I will start painting for sure. I was back drinking coffee and smoking cigarettes at 11:23 p.m. I went and sat on the couch and stared at the paint on the coffee table and the blank white canvas leaning against the wall. The movie Three Amigos came on AMC at midnight. By 2 a.m. I had yet to pick up the brush nearby and use it on the blank white canvas still leaning against the wall. At 2:16 a.m. I decided to go and masturbate. I gave up on painting anything after I finished busting a nut at 2:54 a.m. I took a piss and popped a zit on my nose at 3:12 a.m. By 3:32 a.m. I was lying in bed watching CNN. I set the TV alarm for 15 minutes at 3:45 a.m. I was sleeping soon after.

+++

I was walking home drunk down Moreland Avenue around three in the morning recently. I only had five bucks on me so a cab was out of the question, and I really had no one to call to come get me either. I heard footsteps behind me for quite a while. I finally got paranoid enough that I saw a small brick fence and I sat down and lit a cigarette. A middle aged black man approached me. He asked me how I was doing. I said "Pretty good, but this fucking walk is killing me." He reached into his jacket and pulled out a scratched up faded gold wristwatch. He asked if I would give him five bucks for it. I said "What the fuck" and reached into my pants and pulled out a crisp five dollar bill and handed it to him. He said "Fuck yea, now I can get some Thunderbird!" I put the watch on my right hand and finished walking home. I noticed the next day that the watch didn't work and it smelled funny.

+++

The pigs of hell are circling

Blood dripping from a brown head on a stake

No one notices

Crows and vultures are preparing with knives of nature

Torn flesh

Muscle protruding

Foam and bone await their release

No stitches or antibiotics

Can save you now

Say you're sorry and we might let you in

Streets of gold are calling for you

Even though streets of mud were all you knew

Here

As cries go unheard like the drop of a pin

You are truly free my friend

I'm jealous

The beauty can't be described

+++

I'm sick of being poor. I really am. Twenty-six years so far of scraping by and just having enough to pay the rent. The top five percent have all the luck. They have the money, the power, the jet setting lifestyle, and the hot women. It's funny though, most of the time it's all a result of whose crotch you were ripped out of. George Bush is perfect evidence of this statement. Very few of these people make it on their own. The people that did are usually really skinny lame dorky guys like Bill Gates. Rich people hand the wealth down over the years and through the generations, that's how it works. Perfect examples of this are fucking idiots like Paris Hilton, who is a completely useless human being. I call it the crotch lottery. Some people get it all, and the other ninety-seven percent of the population gets the fucking shaft.

+++

Fuck you tooth! You little son of a bitch motherfucker! I need a pair of pliers to rid myself of you. Do it yourself dental surgery, that's the ticket. I drank all night and still you hurt me. I downed PBR after PBR to get rid of you. I even walked to the gas station and bought two headache powders and downed them, yet still you were there. My head was pulsating. It's going to explode I can feel it. Like a huge zit with a little yellow pus bag coming out of it. FUCK! You have been killing me for months. I fear the dentist and can't really afford it even if I wasn't.

The pain almost puts me on the floor. I paid my tab and left. I went home. I got into the fetal position to wait you out. It still hurts and I can't sleep

+++

It's almost summer again. My mood changes from angst and improves to just antisocial. The people have gotten dumber over the winter it seems. They laugh and say stupid shit to people thinking that they're original and clever. Their fashion is mediocre at best. I can tell people shop at malls here. The guys aren't guys at all in my idea of the word. They're all metrosexual now, popped collars, pastel colors, and too much hair gel. Women love them for some reason. I suppose because of the gay factor. It sickens me. Why can't people just be themselves? I once again reiterate that I was born fifty years too late. The WWII generation would have tolerated none of this bullshit. I miss the days when men were fucking men and didn't spend more time in front of the mirror than their girlfriends.

+++

It hit me like a revelation straight from God himself "Brett you are to get a Pabst Blue Ribbon logo tattooed on your fucking hand." It was commanded and so shall it be done. It will compliment my laziness perfectly. I was getting tired of having to say PBR to all the bartenders and waiters of my usual drinking haunts all the time anyways.

+++

The smell of oil paint fills my room

My ass is numb

I can't move

Without moaning and cursing

A record plays on a distant turntable

Repeatedly

Stains on my shirt are crusting over

Juicy Juice fills a disposable red cup

A cigarette is lit

Inhaled and released to poison the air

Just another late night

Of a disposable soul in the palette of life

+++

With the way men treat women in this town I'm surprised that more women aren't lesbians. I wouldn't blame them if they did switch teams really. People come here and seem to lose what little values and decency they have. Here, it's alright to sexually harass women, and to the untrained eye it would actually seem encouraged. I've been around, more cities and states and countries than I can remember, but the way people act here I can't relate to anywhere else except maybe Panama City. Maybe both places being havens for rednecks on vacation is the answer, I don't really know. These idiots are loud and obnoxious. Being around them gives me a headache and makes me want to stay in my apartment. They litter the town and buy idiotic t-shirts while cleaning out the liquor stores with their fake IDs. Let's all get drunk and have random sex with eighteen year old girls we've known for two hours. Fucking high five motherfucker!

+++

She wanted to kiss me after we finished fucking. I lit a cigarette and turned my head away in disgust.

+++

I crave a deep intelligent conversation, but there isn't one to be found anywhere. From where I sit people are still brutal animals still slowly evolving into human beings. I'm not an elitist I'm just telling the truth. I literally have to put myself into mental cruise control just to be able to relate to people here. I can't think too hard or very much or I will never speak to more than ten people here for months.

+++

Feel free to kill yourself but please don't have any kids

You like Nascar and that's fine

You even voted for Bush two times

Pat Buchanan is correct on race relations

And Bill O'Reilly makes a lot of sense

Feel free to kill yourself but please don't have any kids

Words like "Da club" and "Holla" make up twenty percent of your vocabulary

MTV plays great music

And you have purchased at least one CD by an American Idol contestant

Feel free to kill yourself but please don't have any kids

Reality shows are fantastic and entertaining

You haven't read a book since high school

And think Kapucinski is a country next to Albania

Feel free to kill yourself but please don't have any kids

You spend Thursday nights watching Friends reruns on TBS

America is always right since you live here and you're white

We can win the war on terrorism

Wal Mart is a great place to buy "Stuff"

The levees won't break again

B.C. is a headache powder and not a contraceptive

Feel free to kill yourself but please don't have any kids

Jesus is the one true savior and has a plan for you

Global warming is a myth

Recycling is for pussies

Evolution is a fraud

Abstinence works

Dan Brown writes insightful books you can totally relate to

Dr. Phil is wise and has great advice about your struggling relationship

Feel free to kill yourself but please don't have any kids

+++

Everyday is the same boring repetition for me. I go to bed late and I get up early. I eat around 5 p.m. and that's about it. Eight hours a day slaving for some ultimate fulfillment or accomplishment down the road. It doesn't seem to matter anymore to me. Being there on time or even showing up becomes a daily struggle for me. Despising everyone near you as you walk in the door doesn't help either. I hate them all and I keep to myself, only answering when directly posed a question. Twenty minute bathroom breaks and smoking twice as much just to avoid them and those rooms filled with bad lighting. My mind and body crave more, but they must accept less. Ever get the feeling you've been ripped off by life? Lied to from birth, I was never going to be fucking President of the United States. Depressed and just tired of the doldrums of my everyday life, that's me everyday lately.

+++

I'm tired of technology. I've had enough computers, cell phones, and cable TV to last me the rest of my life. Pretty soon no one will ever have to leave their house for anything. They will stay in and cocoon while the Mexican brick layers take over. One can now go to work or order food and a dildo with a few strokes of the keyboard. What happened to face to face contact, reading books, and writing letters? I say let's get a cup of coffee smoke, some cigarettes, and talk. Fuck your e-mail address and your cell phone, I'm coming over!

+++

This lifestyle is killing me

I've said that same statement

A million times

In my life

Yet it still seems

Fresh

To me

My lifestyle

Is far from glorious

I won't lie about that

But I like it

And I won't

I can't

I refuse

To quit

I'm addicted

A slave to it

No different than crack

Or heroin

I'm no better

Than them

Even though I would like to think

That I am

That would be a lie

As are most things

In life

+++

Me and Mullinax hit Eckerd's drugs hard today. I was on lookout for Mullinax while he grabbed boxes of 1993 Donruss baseball cars and he was on point for me while I stole blank tapes and as much candy as I could stuff down my pants. The fat bald manager kept following us around the store, so we just acted as casually as two juvenile thieves could and browsed near the front of the store. I never though I would actually read the ingredients of sun block, but a thief will do anything to keep a normal consumer profile. We waited for him to ring an old lady up and we headed out the door. The alarm went off as soon as we went by, so we went running as fast as two white boys the age of thirteen could. All our loot was falling out of our pants as we split behind the back of the building. We were laughing the whole time as packs of baseball cards and candy hit the pavement. We jumped into a large green trashcan and shut the little sliding door. We sat there and smoked cigarettes while we waited for the cops to give up on looking for us and split. We ate all the candy and left the cards behind and walked home as innocent as the day we were born.

+++

I'm sorry tourists. I didn't mean it when I said I hated all of your fucking guts and wanted you to die for all those months. It's cold and dark all the time now so you aren't around anymore. I complain when you trash the town I live in and get drunk and act like assholes, but I miss you now, I admit that. When you're around it's hot out. Eighteen year old girls are walking around half naked on the beach and I miss watching. I can't get laid now that you're not around, so I'm back to being a chronic masturbator now. There are no more drunken one night stands with girls from shitty places like Arkansas or Kentucky. Please come back soon my little eighteen year old tourist girls because my cock misses you. I miss the traffic jams and long lines you create at every feasible place. I won't make fun of you for being overweight country white trash idiots anymore, just come back, please. Seeing you ride roller coasters and eating at the Nascar Café always kept me entertained, I admit it now!

+++

I can tell now late in the night picking chunks of vomit out of my teeth that I either shouldn't have drank so much, or I shouldn't have eaten on the way home at that twenty-four hour Dunkin Donuts. I'm too drunk to clean up the vomit. I attempt it, but I keep dropping the roll of toilet paper I was trying to clean it up with. I fall into the cast iron bathtub and can't move. This is the true drunk's bed where we all end up at one time or another.

+++

Before the PBR

I was repulsed by you

Your stomach jiggled even as you sat still

I watched it move

And wanted to throw up

You devoured that plate of chicken wings

Like a school of piranha

Hands covered in orange sauce

And dripping from your obese chin

After the PBR

We were fucking

In the backseat of my Jeep

As the night slowly turned to day

+++

I guess Tim didn't like me very much because today when I went into my boss Bill's office he said I was riding with these guys Johnny and Hubie today. I made small amounts of chit-chat on the ride over to an abandoned middle school where we would be working at. But mostly, I smoked cigarettes and read my newspaper in the back of the van which is where I was sitting with all the tools and machines and shit. They made me fetch shit all day. They called me a "Go-pher." I guess it's a clever little plumber's joke or something. I didn't mind though, it was sure better than being under the house in the crawlspace again. But of course I knew it wouldn't last, after lunch I got to dig a ditch for the rest of the day. I'm just a white nigger I guess. For some reason Johnny tried to convince me that Huey Lewis was the greatest guitar player in the world. I think this guy is retarded or something, but we'll see.

+++

Hitting the iron again

Makes me feel strong and invincible

My saggy tits tighten up over time

My stomach reduces and the fat doesn't protrude anymore

I am suddenly strong in body and mind once again

Animal instincts take over

People's conversations become blurry to me

I know I could strangle someone, anyone with my bare fucking hands

I could hurt people possibly

And I like knowing that there's a chance I could

If not that, at least my pants fit better

I beat my dick furiously now

And the cum fills the wad of toilet paper completely

Where as before it just sort of dribbled out

All I need now is a woman to try it out on

Which is easier said than done

When you're an anti social loner

And have no skills at all with them

The years of PBR, frozen pizzas, and cartons of cigarettes

Are being shredded away slowly

No, I haven't stopped those things

And I never will probably

The iron gives me resistance to their calls of procrastination

On Saturday and Sundays

The only thing that was missing has been found again

Now that I'm hitting the iron again

+++

The only way to achieve true freedom in its most basic form is to round up every cop and military personnel and shoot them in the face. Without the iron fist of control our government would cease to dictate any authority over us. Thomas Jefferson and Sam Adams would have already tried this if they were alive today. They would now be rotting in jail awaiting execution on grounds of being "Terrorists." I just hope I live long enough to see our global empire known as America fall. It would probably the greatest thing that has happened to the overall world in a century. We would not like it of course, but those oppressed and dying from our control in foreign countries wouldn't mind it one bit. It's going to happen, realize that. All the great dynasties have fallen, from Egypt to Rome to the Greeks. It's just a matter of time people. So watch all the MTV you can now and buy those Jessica Simpson CDs quick, because one day I'll be using them as firewood when this motherfucker burns. All I know is that me and Ted Nugent are going to be alright, but the majority of you are going to be fucked though.

+++

It's 2:09 p.m.

On a cold

Saturday afternoon

My lemon lime Gatorade sits to my right

Half full and reeking of bad stale breath

My teeth are unbrushed

My armpits begin to stink badly

Snot is spit into a plastic red cup to my left

The deodorant sits nearby in my bathroom

But it's ten feet too far from me

Maybe I will get there when I have to take a piss later

I have three cigarettes left

But a whole pack I bought last night awaits me in the car

I can't imagine even going out there right now

I can't go out there naked

So I have to put it off for now

I will smoke the filters in my ashtray before I go out there

The sun will be too much

I like my dark room too much to leave

I like my gray chair too much to move

I like my three cigarettes

And my lemon lime Gatorade sitting to my right

They're all I need right now

They may be all I need for the rest of the day

Or even for the rest of the night

Until it's time to put on last night's clothes

And go get fucked up

Once again

They're all this white boy needs for right now

+++

I find myself lonelier than ever. Most of the time I'm cool with it but once in a while it does get to me. I just want to feel normal for a little bit. It never seems that way though. I talk to less and less people it seems. I'm tired of feeling like a slob. It's time to hit it hard. More writing, painting, drinking and fucking will do me good. It seems like there's less and less to do these days. Fuck being outside right now, it's forty-three degrees and raining out there. I'm missing the summer and the people watching for sure. It's so odd, I hate people but I like watching them, it's a real catch twenty-two I guess. Why go to the movies when people are the real fiction.

+++

I was having a good old time in the bar until I ordered all those Long Island Ice Tea's and then ate that cheeseburger and tater tots after. Thirty minutes later I walked outside the front door of the Highlander and vomited all over the sidewalk and all on my shoes as well. My friend Frank and his girlfriend found me in the fetal position some time later in the parking lot. He asked how I was feeling. I said "Just peachy" as I proceeded to puke all over a small tree nearby. He and his girlfriend laughed at me. That's the last thing I remember about that night.

+++

I'm going on two hours of sleep. I just had sex twice in less than five hours. Of course, I had to go through a bunch of bullshit to do that though. Sometimes getting laid isn't even worth the trouble! After what seemed like an eternity of foreplay, she was still hesitant to fuck me. At around six in the morning I told her to fuck off and I went and slept on the couch. Two minutes later, I had to take a huge piss so I had to go back into my room to go to the bathroom. She actually apologized to me when I went in there. God, women are fucking stupid! I did end up fucking this girl finally. We started out with a Trojan condom, but of course being completely drunk, I couldn't cum, so after an hour the condom came off. It felt great; condoms really do ruin sex for me. I think Eazy E said it best "I was born in the pussy and I'll die in the pussy," or some shit like that, but, then again, he did die of AIDS so maybe that isn't the wisest advice I've ever heard. Her fucking phone kept ringing all morning, but I was too lazy to get up and throw it against the wall. After a while I couldn't sleep so I slipped it in her pussy once again. This new picture phone I just bought really paid off. I was like some fucked up perverted version of Martin Scorcese. She had a foul mouth as well, which I do enjoy. Phrases like "I want your big cock inside me" and "I want you to cum all over my face" were uttered during the "Session." How can any guy hear shit like that and not just cum on the spot? This victim was pretty cool, I'll admit. She didn't even try and cuddle with me which was a pleasant surprise. Cuddling makes me want to kill with extreme prejudice. I smoked a cigarette while she took a shower. I drove her home after that, and I dropped her off at some shitty looking apartments on 38th Avenue.

She asked me if I wanted to come in and see her dog. I said I had to go and I got the hell out of there. I'll never call her again unless I'm pretty hard up. Chalk up another victim.

+++

Vincent was a pussy. All he could muster the courage for was an ear. Paul wasn't that impressed, and neither am I. Vincent should have cut off his cock instead. That would have made more of an impression on Paul I do believe.

+++

I'm ready to escape this town. There's nothing but heartbreak and bad memories here. There are a few good memories yes, but not as many as there should be. I hope this little escape to Atlanta clears my head. I'll try not to be bored and lonely like I am in Myrtle Beach all the time. Hanging out with old friends and seeing Slayer on Thanksgiving Day should do the trick. It's now three weeks until I leave for Europe and I'm trying hard to contain my excitement, but I can't. This has been a long time coming!

+++

Budweiser is all a man needs. You're the one friend that doesn't disappoint me on a constant basis. I know what I get from you. You're the beautiful brown hottie with the red label. I love what you do for me. You get me laid. You make me have fun. You make me do really dumb things. You give me confidence where none exists. But you also give me headaches and make me feel like dying. It's an even trade-off in the end.

+++

We had plans to meet up around 10 p.m. tonight. You never showed up though. What did I expect, someone to change or become a different person in a month? That's idiotic and I know better; but I did it anyways. I drove home alone and felt like a loser the whole time. I fantasized blowing you off the next time to get revenge for this, but we know this will never happen. All I can do is fantasize about it and have epic dreams of sweet revenge. The only thing that brought me any comfort at all that day was reading the newspaper while taking a big shit when I got home.

+++

The fall air brings with it the depression. The alienation is slowly mounting. It's cold outside and I have nothing to do. I want to go for a walk, but there are no real streets here to get lost on. There are only subdivisions and nosy neighbors around here.

+++

I'm so fucking horny today. I called up a girl that I fucked the other week. She's got serious problems, but then again, women that I get involved with always do for some reason. I called and left a message. I guess I will sit here a few hours and then masturbate if she doesn't call me back. I need to fuck something now, there's no time to wait. I'm like a rabid fucking animal. I want to cum on someone's face, call her a whore, and fucking leave!

+++

Forced entries into a black notebook

Sweat drips from a forehead

It's hotter than hell and

The headache is still there

But my mind keeps swirling

Putting hotel room pen onto lined white paper

Isn't as easy as you might think

People and bullshit keep me distracted

You can't avoid them all of the time

Human beings are such horrible social creatures

What an affliction to possess

+++

I was fingering a girl in a parking lot. Her goo was all over my fingers. It was amazing how I managed to get my hand down her tight jeans and into her pussy; it was almost a magic trick Houdini would have been proud of. I even talked her into letting me put it in her butt while I was fingering her. We were both drunk. I told her to follow me, which she did, until we got to the first light. She stopped on yellow, the dumb bitch. I tried to pull over and wait for her but I couldn't change lanes. I told her to meet me at a bar near my house, so I assumed she would know that was the place to go if we got separated. I waited for what felt like an hour in my car about to piss my pants. I realized she wasn't going to show. I turned my car back around and headed back to the bar we met at, checking the gas stations and restaurants on the way for her car. It was nowhere to be found. I didn't have her number so I was basically fucked. I decided to go home. Once again, life does what it can to keep me from even the slightest bit of happiness. I jerked off twice and went to bed when I got home.

+++

Women and politicians have a lot in common. I know nothing about either except for the fact that you can't trust them for shit. But, somehow, I end up playing ball. I love and vote; therefore, I am truly a fool for the ages.

+++

I often want to ask my father why he even had me. All the years of beatings and degradation did take a little toll on me. Being called a "Loser" "Worthless" "Stupid son of a bitch" and, the best of all, the "I wish you were never born" line still fuck with me on occasion. These are all an assortment of things said to me since I can remember. They are still with me to this day, always in the back of my mind hiding somewhere. I remember bottles of Jack Daniels lying around the house and being clubbed until I bled with anything your drunken ass could manage to grab. The fishing pole and the bat were my favorites. I cry as I write this, if that is proof enough Dad, you have reduced a grown man to tears all these years later. It never made sense to me, but I deal with it. It's hard to believe all these years later the memories are still with me. Being unloved and abused since the day you were born can take a mental and physical toll on you. I'm still recovering and trying to find myself in it somewhere. This lifestyle I was born into forced me to be stronger, to be able to take more and still survive. I am the cockroach you can't fucking kill, I will be here when you're gone.

+++

I woke up in the middle of the night and stabbed you. I wiped off the knife on that set of kitchen towels your Mom gave us for Christmas and I put it back in the drawer. Since the bed was messy, I got my sleeping bag out of the closet and passed out on the couch. Maybe now I can get some peace and quite for once.

+++

I know that I will die alone and miserable. If more people acknowledged that they were as well, the world would be a better place.

+++

Masturbation

I'm in love with my hand

A touch of lotion and

You're better than some women

I've had

A small ball of toilet paper to

Catch my love of the ages

A few footsteps to the toilet

A flush and you disappear forever

There's no talking or holding after

Just the act and it's over

The way it should be

+++

I went to Wal Mart today and bought a piece of luggage with wheels on it. Now I'll look like a pussy-ass banker or something in the airport with my luggage that I carry around behind me like a ball and chain. It's better to carry that than a woman, I guess. My trip to Amsterdam is at hand and I can't wait.

+++

I can't sleep. The neighbors below me wake me up on Sunday at 7:12 a.m. with the sounds of loud bass rattling my entire room. I hear the music and then I hear them screaming at their kids. They make me dislike fat black people. I get pissed and call them "Niggers." I jerk off hoping that will help. I clean up my little wad of toilet paper I use to catch the cum with, and then I lay back down in my bed. I wake up again at 9:03 a.m. and I can't go back to bed. I jerk off again hoping that this will be the one that sends me into deep REM sleep. I lay back down once again. This time, I just roll around and feel the bass but I can't sleep once again. I grab my bedspread and go lay on the couch. I wake up again at 11:26 a.m. They turned the volume up, so now I really can't sleep and I'm getting pissed. I jerk off once again. The cum volume produced by me was pathetic and my dick is all shriveled up now from the mass abuse, I was spent. I bring my bedspread back into my room and lay down once again. I laid there thinking of all the fucked up things I want to do to them for keeping me up on a Sunday morning. If the hangover wasn't bad enough this just makes it unbearable. I think of going down there naked and knocking on the door, walking past the fat black woman and her kids and grabbing the PA system that they must have down there to produce such a volume sound that it rattles my apartment and raising it above my head and smashing it to the floor. I would give an evil little laugh and then take a piss in the corner of the room just for spite. Damn, if I only had the balls to do it.

+++

I can't wait until I get cancer. I smoke enough cigarettes that I can pretty much guarantee myself that it will happen, and I can't wait. I will finally have the freedom to truly live life. How interesting would it be to know pretty much when you're going to die? It's like God fucked up somewhere and I found a loophole in the system. I would find everyone that was cruel and inhumane to me during my life and exact revenge. I would play God! How much sweeter would it be with them being completely void of what was going to happen to them. It would probably go down as a random crime, but I would know better. Once I got the call about the cancer, I would sit down in my living room and make my little list up. I would have to find past yearbooks from the high school I went to for a short time and look for names and pictures. Those football players ten times bigger than me that harassed me every day for no reason would get it for sure; and maybe even their families as well. My Dad would definitely get a bullet. Although, I might spare him and only blow out his kneecaps so he would have to be in a wheelchair the rest of his life. That cop that was a dick to me the other day would get it, hell, as many cops as I could find would get it. The neighbor's downstairs would get it, and so would their fucking stereo. That's all I have on my yellow sheet of lined notebook paper at the moment. It will take me a while to brainstorm and come up with more names, give me a fucking break, I just started it.

+++

Getting caught was never in the back of their minds like it was mine. To me, it seemed alright and reasonable to steal little things, but I rarely took part in the big schemes. Drug and grocery stores were our favorite spots to hit. We stole anything we could get our hands on. This is just the way it was since none of us ever had any money. We would steal beer and cigarettes from the gas station, baseball cards and condoms from the drug stores, and all our electronics from Wal Mart.

+++

Golf is not a sport. At best it's really a hobby like bowling or pool just without the fun. Oh, but you take it so seriously don't you HONKEY? You whine and cry if there's any sort of noise while you're swinging that little iron club. The whole world should be quiet on your whim when you're swinging that little club HONKEY. Get drunk and cheat on your score card to make yourself feel better HONKEY. If you play golf, I hate your guts HONKEY! Could you be any whiter? What possesses you to dress like an idiot and ride little motorized carts around pristine land that could house numerous 7-Elevens or cheap apartment buildings for bums like me to live in HONKEY?

+++

I stare in the mirror and don't know who or what

I am anymore

I'm part animal

Man

And machine

Organic matter and atoms spliced

A dash of self hate

And a pinch of neuroticism

And I'm a complete meal

This world

My world

Slowly rots away from tooth decay

Why even try and save this piece of shit place

Extract all of it

The people are the worst and ruin it all

Extract them to save it maybe

Without the Novocain

It will never happen though

Only the greats and the originals go down

And are easily forgotten

Darwinism placed on hold

In a never ending long distance phone call

Between George Bush and David Duke

+++

She unzips my pants as I press buttons on a black remote. Her head disappears into my lap. I light a cigarette and sip on my drink. I watch as the streetlight casts shadows on the side of her face through my cheap white blinds. Time passes slowly.

"What the fuck's wrong with you?' she asks.

"What do you mean?" I reply.

"Do I not do it for you or something?"

"Am I not hot or something?"

"Your dick is limp, what am I doing here?"

"I'm sorry, baby."

"You know it was hard at first, I don't know what's wrong now."

"You're a waste of my time," she replies.

She gathered her shoes and purse and split out the front door as fast as she could. I just sat on the couch smoking my cigarette and finishing my drink. What can you really do in a situation like this?

'Fuck that bitch" I say to myself.

"I know it will work, she just didn't know what she was doing."

I go into my room and turn on whatever crappy porn tape was in my VCR at the time and I started jerking off. The next thing I knew, I was woken up by my roommate Kelly the next morning, with my pants around my ankles and my dick in my hand. What a loser I've become.

+++

As lame as suicide might first appear to be, it's actually a pretty ballsy thing to do I think. As much as I say that it's fucked up and wrong, I'm curious about it. It fucked with me and hurt when several friends of mine did it over the years. David hung himself in a tree and Bob woke up one morning and ate a gun. That was so fucking insane at the time that I couldn't figure out why they would do it. What was the final breaking point? Damn, they did have the nerve though. To sit there with a loaded gun, nervous and sweating, knowing that this moment was the last time you would take a breath or see your Mom again or get laid took some amount of nerve. I wish I had their guts. So when I hear people talk about how cowardly an act like that is, I always want to correct their ignorance. I want to say "Hey, you would never have the balls to end your shit like that." It's a fucked up thing that I don't recommend anyone doing, but it interests me.

+++

I don't know where all my cynicism came from. I came from a fucked up background, granted, but so do a lot of people. And a lot of people had it a million times worse than I did growing up. For all the good things that it does for me, sometimes I wish it wasn't there. The "Normal" life by society's standards could probably be had by me then. The job that pays the bills but that I secretly hate could be mine. The wife or girlfriend asking me how my day was when I came home could also be mine for the taking. Kids and family vacations to Disneyworld would also be attainable for me, but there will be none of that for me. I'm set in my ways now. My life works for me I guess. The cynicism keeps me alone and at a distance from people sometimes. I want to apologize for being fucked up, but I can't help it. I guess high school is where it began. While everyone was getting cars for their sixteenth birthdays, I was riding a skateboard. While other people were going on dates and sexually exploring, I was a chronic masturbator. I was the weird looking guy wearing crappy clothes and cutting my own crooked mohawks. I was not exactly the guy that any respectable girl wanted to hang out with. I sat at the loser table in the lunchroom along with my fellow nerds, metal heads, potheads, skaters, and pretty much anyone else that wasn't classifiable as "Preppy, jock, or popular." For as much as that period of my life sucked, it taught me a lot of lessons. I can almost guarantee that the kids at the loser table became much better human beings in the end than anyone whose sole existence in life was to be beautiful and popular.

+++

Disgusted by humanity

I'm sorry the lack of one

Violence doesn't solve violence

But no one in power remembers that

All they know is death, starvation, embargoes

Gulags, wars, and oppression

Rarely does that ever change

For every one Martin Luther King there are ten

Joseph Stalin

People have been blind so long

Stevie Wonder was even impressed

I hope they wake up soon

But I fear it might be too late

Bush

And those gutless green paper whores

In the House and Senate

Have a few more years to

Fuck everything up

More then they already have

+++

Here I sit at the Greyhound Bus Terminal at 6:34 in the morning. I got here around 5 a.m. and I found the cleanest bench I could find to sit down on. An old homeless lady wearing ratty clothes is sleeping on the bench across from me. A few buses come and go but not many. I hear the announcement overhead for buses leaving for Detroit and Chicago and a few people scurry along and file into the white and blue buses of steel. I watch them pull out, and I know I will be on one soon. It's now 7:15 a.m. and my girl was supposed to show up fifteen minutes ago but she's still not here. We're catching the 7:45 a.m. bus to Memphis. We plan on getting married by an Elvis impersonator when we get there, and start a new life for ourselves and escape this ghetto shithole of a town where nothing seems to be going right. I quit my job a few days ago and collected my last check and packed a few things and here I sit with all of my possessions in a black industrial strength garbage bag. I wait a few minutes and then dig some change out of the bottom of my pant's pocket and I give my baby a call. The phone rings five times before there's an answer. A strange voice answers the phone.

"Hello?" I ask.

The manly voice answers "Who the fuck is this?"

"Do you know what time it is?"

"Where is Jennifer?" I ask.

"What the fuck happened to her?"

"Where the fuck is Jen?"

There is a pause on the phone for a few seconds.

"Brett is that you?" a soft voice answers.

"Yea, it's me baby."

"I'm down here at the bus station where are you?"

"You were supposed to be here twenty minutes ago."

"Brett, we broke up two months ago."

"You really need to get over this" she says.

"I fucking love you, don't you understand this?" I reply.

"You're the only girl I want, the only one for me."

"Get dressed and go to Memphis with me."

"I love you."

There is another pause on the phone. The male voice comes on the phone again

"Dude, get a fucking life."

"Jen doesn't want you anymore fuckface!"

"If you bother her anymore, I'm gonna kick your fucking ass."

I hear a click on the other end of the phone. I just stand there for a second in shock. What about our new life? That bitch said that she would love me forever. I guess a month is forever sometimes. I hear the announcement "Last call to Memphis." I walk over to the bench I was sitting on and sat down for a second. The old homeless lady in the ratty clothes had woken up. I walk over to her and handed her my extra ticket to Memphis and said "Hey what are you doing for the rest of your life beautiful?" We gather our matching black garbage bags and step on the bus hand in hand. Life is funny like that sometimes.

+++

A past revisited

The woman does it to me

What can I say?

I might regret punching in those

Drunken numbers

Feeling foolish doing it didn't

Stop me at all

I don't mind being a complete idiot

This is obvious by

Most of my actions apparently

Drunken cell phone dialing

The new regret of the 21st century

+++

Can we sell Paris Hilton to China? I would respect her much more if she worked twelve hours a day in a sweatshop making Nike shoes. I want to see pictures of her wearing rags and being flogged every time she messes up a stitch line. They can put the pictures of her in Maxim so I have something new to jerk off to next month.

+++

The streets of Amsterdam are amazing at night. The cobblestone streets carry you casually through this ancient city. It's so peaceful and quiet here at night that I don't even mind or notice the cold rain falling on me. I pass a couple on the canal kissing under a tree and I'm jealous of them for a minute. I can see a hotel's blue lights at a distance. I'm a world away from where I come from and I revel in every second of it. To live and die here must be glorious I would think.

+++

Today, instead of going home after my nine hours of manual labor, I went to a bar near my house. It was a low class bar indeed. They didn't even carry imported beer, just domestic. Everyone drank Miller High Life or PBR anyways, so to have anything else would have been a waste of time. I was sitting there watching "The game" on TV. Well I should say I was staring at the TV but not really paying any attention to what was going on. Two black guys came in and sat down on the stools next to me. I sat there for a while sipping my beer and saying nothing. I overheard one of the black men say that he'd like to get his hands on some fat white girl's ass. I laughed as I heard them talking.

I said "Man, trust me, if you ever had any white girl ass, you wouldn't want it again."

"Hey, if you don't believe me, here's the keys to apartment number eight over on Dixie Avenue where I live."

"Go fuck my lard ass of a wife, I don't care."

"Are you serious?"

"Fuck yea, I'm serious man."

"Tag team that bitch and make her scream."

"But make sure you punch her in the face as soon as she asks how your day was."

"That's my only commandment."

I took the key to my apartment and handed it to the large black man next to me and said "You boys have fun now." I ordered another beer and high fived the bartender as the Braves scored another run.

+++

I kiss your lips softly. A bulge grows in my pants. It stabs you in the stomach as I lift you onto the hood of my car. Our mouths move to the right and to the left. I take your spit and slobber into my mouth and return the favor. My hand slides near the center of your dress. I can feel the heat of it on my hand. A security guard pulls up next to us and tells us to "Take that shit somewhere else you perverts!"

+++

Today was a really strange day. I woke up at eight today and zoned out for a while. I somehow managed to get dressed and all that. My brother, who was still somewhat drunk from the night before, drove me to the dentist's office. I downed a bunch of pills and they gave me a shot in my right arm directly in my "Slip it in" tattoo. I started to feel a little funny at this point, after that everything is a blank. I don't remember how the hell I got home. The next thing I knew, I woke up lying on my New Kids on The Block beach towel catching some rays at my pool. I wandered around for a minute and then I walked to my apartment. I looked around, and then asked myself why there was now five vanilla Frappuccinos, a pack of light bulbs, a newspaper, a Lion King cup with a huge bloody tooth in it next to a bottle of Vicodin on my table.

+++

Cups filled with spit and urine line my nightstand

No need

Or the will to stumble into the bathroom anymore

The last time I did

I pissed all over the floor anyway

Cigarette packs and phone numbers

Written on white bar napkins

Litter the floor near my bed

Stained underwear worn

Twice before and later tonight

Are still inside my pants

Frozen pizza boxes and dirty plates

Welcome visitors into my

Humble abode

Instead of a "Welcome" mat

Mine should read

"Lazy fucking slob" and have an arrow

Pointing this way

+++

People leave towns for lots of different reasons I suppose. I leave towns when I can't go anywhere in public and not see a girl I have fucked before or a girl that hates my guts. This is when I know it's time to find a new suitable destination for my cooterific empire. I'm only kidding though, or am I?

+++

I crack a joke and I feel better

Temporarily

My stomach turns to knots

When she gave me a hug and kissed me

On the cheek

I raised my hand in the direction of my waiter

"Another vodka please."

Wearing shorts during winter

Random

Ronnie James Dio

Plays on the jukebox in Hell

+++

When on a perfect week long drinking binge many things in life become clear. Time, for all real purposes loses value. As do dates, appointments, and schedules. Basic human survival instinct mode kicks in. When it gets dark, it's time to drink again. When you wake up, you wake up. There's no need for an alarm clock since all you're going to do is just nurse yourself back enough to fill your body once again with booze and cigarettes. Conversations become more neurotic. Your head is constantly cloudy and details lose their luster. You become a true babbling idiot with no clear coherent message. The only message I think people understand is that you're a fucking scumbag drunk. It appears that bartenders can sense these things, but the average person I might talk to in a bar probably confuses this for general psychotic activity. I wake up every morning feeling like I got ran over by a train. I shit about four or five times throughout the day. Food is not really needed, only the occasional frozen pizza when I come home drunk at four in the morning. I've worn the same pants for five days straight now. They have the aroma of stale cigarettes and rotting beer. My stomach hurts, my teeth are brown, and most of my fingers are yellow. All I have to do is make it one more night. I have it in me, I think. This will be my same message tomorrow probably.

+++

Hiding under a hat and hooded sweatshirt

So no one notices me parking or going into

That porn store on Business 17

Black bag in hand

A few minutes later

I hope the drive-thru guy at Arby's

Doesn't notice that I'm a fucked up pervert

A large roast beef sandwich and super sized curly fry please

Fills the air in my car in four minutes and twelve seconds

I light another cigarette to pass the time

Only a few minutes until I'm eating

Fast food on the couch alone

And playing with my cock until I'm bored

Or run out of cum

+++

I spent almost seven hours under an old abandoned house over in East Atlanta today. At first the smell of cat piss and bugs crawling on me bothered me a little, but after a few hours I got used to it. I had my little piece of plastic I rolled onto the floor to try and keep some of the dirt off of me. It made for a fine pillow bunched up throughout the day though. Tim, my co-worker, was outside all day handing me shit I needed for the water pipes I was ripping out. After lunch, in the right darkest corner, I found a used syringe. I observed it for a while with my flashlight since I didn't have anything else to do. I guess a junky crawled under here at one point and shot up. Being the new guy at work really fucking sucks, that's all I fucking know at this point.

+++

It's 3:38 in the morning. I'm not tired so there's no need to sleep. Tomorrow is a long day so I would rather be tired and out of it, half awake and out of it makes it more bearable. I sit here alone, feeling lonely. The TV fills no void so I turn it off. It was a shitty movie about Vietnam anyway. I'm sick of hearing about war so there's no need to watch movies about it when it's happening everyday. It's the reason I have since stopped reading my usual newspaper. It's nothing but a waste of time lately anyways. I sit here staring at the wall smoking a cigarette. I'm thinking too much tonight. I'm feeling weak and trying to make sense of things, but it's not really happening, not that it ever does. I love these nights of complete and utter solitude as much as I hate them. As I've stated before, it's not for everyone. I've got more stories and writing ideas floating around in my head dying to come out. They force me here. Hands pressing little square black keys are my soundtrack to the angst. I occasionally stare at the crack of light under the door. My four walls might as well be a part of my body now. I know every angle, every mistake, and every stain. The dirty clothes in the corner are as familiar to me as my face. The bed, the ruler, the desk, the CD rack, the weights; I know them all like best friends. They are the only constant and my only companions on nights like these.

+++

I spotted a fat girl from my window today. She must live below me somewhere. She was carrying bags of groceries in as I lifted the blinds and started stroking my cock.

+++

Sitting on the stairs while a storm approaches from the West

An airplane goes over my head

Horizontal rain hits me in the face

And forces a retreat inside my four walls

Firecrackers wake me from a peaceful sleep

An erection keeps me up

Jerking off puts me down again

A gun enters my mouth

I eat a bullet for breakfast

That's how I start everyday

+++

I squeeze you as hard as I could. My face turned blood red and hurt. You wouldn't wave your white flag or repent your ways. A lit needle would be your demise. Soaked in alcohol to make you burn. I poked you with my sharp toy of destruction a few times and squeeze some more. Your yellow kingdom of pus has been conquered and evicted from my face. Your new home shall be the sewer of paradise.

+++

I woke up and you were gone. At least I thought you were. I looked out the window and spotted your Volkswagen in the parking lot. I walked back into my room and double checked to see if in my hazy awakening I had overlooked you somewhere. You weren't there. I looked in the bathroom, the kitchen, and even in the shower, but you were nowhere to be found. I finally walked through the living room and onto the porch. There you were sitting in my plastic white chair. I opened the sliding glass door and "Hi," but there was no answer from you. I walked in front you and saw that you had your eyes closed. I shook you, but you didn't wake up. I noticed my cutting board on the table next to you covered in small white dust and a rolled up dollar bill lying next to it. A small amount of blood trickled from your nose as I walked away.

+++

I had just pulled into the parking lot of my favorite local drinking hole. There was nowhere to park, so I ended up having to park down the street. The fact that I live in a beach town and this was September, all the parking meters had been taken up so I found a nice spot with just a black pole sticking out of the ground. I found my cigarettes and a blue lighter in my dashboard. I took a gulp of water and opened my overhead mirror. There were noticeable black bags under my eyes and I pretty much overall looked like hell, but in a dark bar who the hell cares or notices details like that anyways. I flipped the mirror back up and cracked open the door and placed my feet on the ground. It's show time motherfucker.

+++

"Why won't you make out with me anymore?"

"I don't know."

"I don't really do that anymore, Brett."

"Why not?" I ask.

"Because, I'm too mature for PDA now."

"Yea, I don't blame you."

"I always wondered why you made out with me anyways."

"Frankly, you're way out my league."

"No, I'm not Brett."

"Well you don't have to say it but I know the real truth."

"How about we go outside and make out then?"

"That way it really won't be technically PDA."

"Nice try Brett, but no."

+++

I held your hair

As you vomited into the sink

You couldn't even make it to

The toilet anymore

Green mucus flows from your

Track marks

Making their way past the scabs

I'm just a passenger on your

Train of self destruction

It's the true form of evolution

Withered and pale

The transformation of true beauty

To complete ugliness

I respect that about you

+++

I was so broke today that I had to pay for my #3 McDonald's combo meal in change that I found under the mat and in the seats of my car. Surprisingly, nothing seemed out of order when I pulled up to the drive-thru window and I handed the wad of dirt and lint filled copper and nickel change to the attendant and grinned.

+++

Men seem to be continually concerned about their dick size. I don't think this was brought about or could be blamed on women in any way. Most that have seen my small one never made a big deal about it. Who knows, maybe they talked shit to their friends afterwards and I don't about it, but does that really count if I'm ignorant to it? No, I think we as human beings enjoy the need to worry about shit that shouldn't be worried about. There's not much you can do about it anyways, so why care? I blame some company trying to make a few bucks to sell some useless pills or some new radical surgical technique developed in Paraguay or some fucking place. But just to bring a new rationale to this debate, I bring up my newly developed theory. Maybe guys don't have small penises after all. Maybe some women just have really big vaginas. It's just a thought.

+++

Coming home to my apartment, I know what's waiting for me when I pull in. As always, they are there. No matter the time or day, they are always there in the parking lot yelling and screaming and getting on my nerves. I dread going outside now. I don't go to the pool anymore. I don't ride my bike anymore. I don't go for walks anymore. Everything I do out there is precise and quick now. I don't want to answer anymore stupid questions or hear them in general. I never wished children death before, until now.

+++

Two gigabytes for self and love

The W is next to the E

The only way I can handle it

Five-hundred miles away from it

The J is next to the H

The white screen in front of me

Keeping my eyes red and clean

A few clicks and you're there in my room

From five-hundred miles away

The C is next to the V

It's the only relationship to have

In my room but five-hundred miles away

The bullshit and drama ends with

A click

The I is next to the U

Then you're gone again

Until I'm lonely and weak

And the depression kicks in heavy

The S is next to the A

A few right clicks and you're there again

Once more

The M is next to the N

Love, Netflix, and Domino's pizza

Just a right or left click away in the 21st century

+++

The process of removing my cock from a vagina and then somehow making it to her face before I cum is quite the impossible act. I always end up cumming on her tits or neck before I get up there. Maybe one day I will climb that mountain.

+++

My friend John called me up and said he was house sitting for his sister while she was out of town. I took the Marta train up to North Atlanta and walked the rest of the way. We fucked around and watched TV for a while, but we had out minds set on getting drunk tonight. Getting away from your parents and having somewhere to crash was a rare event, so we had to make it count. We headed down to the Amoco gas station and hung around smoking cigarettes waiting for the right looking kind of person to score us some beer. We flipped a coin and I lost, so it was my job to go up to people and ask them if they would hook us up with anything. Twenty people probably went by before I thought I saw someone worth asking. I went up to a group of black guys in an Oldsmobile but none of them wanted to do it for the three extra bucks I had to offer them. I went back to the curb and sat down again. Another fifteen minutes went by and then I saw another possibility. I saw two young white guys with two really hot girls in the car with them. I asked the first white guy I saw and he said sure no problem. He asked me what I wanted and I said a case of Icehouse. I handed him a ten-dollar bill and headed back over to the curb. The guy was in the store for a few minutes and then he came out carrying our case of cheap American booze. I ran over to him and he handed it to me. I told him to keep the change but he said not to worry about it. I waved goodbye to the girls inside the car and we walked back up the street to the apartment. We started chugging beers like there was no tomorrow. I was drunk and stumbling before I knew it. I hadn't eaten all day so it wasn't long before I was out on the porch puking all over his sister's bushes in front of the apartment. I've never had that much shit come out of me at any one time in my entire life. I swear two weeks of past food came out along with all of the Icehouse. I went into the bathroom to clean up and take a shit. I read a Glamour magazine which was the only reading material in the bathroom. For some unknown reason I decided to jerk off while I was in there. I found a jar of petroleum jelly underneath the sink and flipped the pages of the Glamour magazine until I had a hard on. I came to a picture of a Cindy Crawford perfume ad. I don't know how, but I did. I shot my cum in my little wad of toilet paper that I had and left it in the toilet and stumbled out and into the couch. John went into the bathroom later on and came out accusing me of jerking off in his sister's bathroom. I played it cool, like I had no idea what he was talking about. But I guess the wad of toilet paper, the jar of petroleum jelly, and the opened Glamour magazine gave me away. He yelled at me to get in there and clean my mess up, but I just said "Fuck you, why don't you clean it up? I'm too drunk right now," all the while laughing my ass off. My friend John was relegated to cleaning up my mess. I passed out on the couch not too long after. We headed down to Waffle House the next day for lunch and neither of us spoke of the incident from the previous night. I walked towards the train station and got the train headed home with the worst hangover I'd ever had in my life. I had to be at my crappy job at McDonalds later that day, what fucking luck!

+++

With serpent's eyes

The flick of a cigarette

Decides our fate

The hesitant switch

Silence disturbed

The sidewalk reigns

The stepfather of time

And the purveyor of discontent

A voyeur's face glows bright as the sun

Disappointment is my deadly sin of addiction

Fate leaves me weak and bewildered

A leper's plea for reconciliation

Of a life once remembered

Good and just actions are

As they say overrated

Obedience

I have lost

A child I remain

Never has a day turned

Without a dream dying

It festers on a branch

In Western Montana

We strip ourselves

Whoring out what internal organs

Donated or sold

A gavel strikes at a distance

Life is over I hear

Is there

Was there

Any point to anything

To any of it

+++

The bar, unlike most other places of social interaction, I truly feel at home. At work, or hell, even in the grocery store, classism exists. There's always that well dressed yuppie character who thinks he doesn't have to wait in line or deserves that bag of Doritos before you do just because you shop in dirty soiled pants and steel-toe boots. Although, the worst people are the rich old housewives who seem to have nothing better to do but to be complete cunts. The bar eliminates class really. Everyone in there are losers and seem to be alright with that fact. It's one of the few places of solace, where for the most part, people can get along. Over the years god knows I've gotten into some fucking strange conversations with a real multitude of various people. Let's be honest here. For the most part, everything people think is really important in life is probably bullshit. We're all just looking for filler, filler of hours until we go to sleep and wake up and do the same shit again that we did the day before. Everything is pointless and redundant at some point but I can think of no other place I would rather be and fill my unimportant life with than the bar.

+++

My old worn out Ramone's black t-shirt

Always there in the closet

But sometimes on the floor

Just depends on how drunk or lazy I am

Cigarette burns

And unknown stains made you

More beautiful

Over all these years

We have been together

+++

It was raining like hell when I pulled into the parking lot at school. I had even cowardly brought out an umbrella that I found earlier in the day in the closet. I hadn't used one in years, but I didn't really feel like being drenched all day so I gave it a shot. The umbrella was pretty much useless with the strong winds that were blowing the rain horizontally. I walked to the front of the building and tossed the small blue umbrella in the trash. I smoked half a cigarette before the clock struck 3 p.m. Damn it! I can't even enjoy a fucking smoke anymore these days. I walked into the half empty class. I saw a seat right next to this girl I had admired in class for sometime now. My eyes flashed around every seat, I hesitated for a second then planted a foot in her direction. I looked at her as I sat down and she smiled back at me. There was one seat between us. I wasn't into what the English teacher was rattling on about so I pulled a book I'd been neglecting out of my bag and opened it up and started reading. After a few minutes, I acted like the chair between us was really getting in my way and kept bumping my elbow every time I turned a page. I put my book on the table and moved the chair back against the wall. I then slowly maneuvered myself a little closer to her. She looked over at me and seemed to give an approval to my actions. We both had a little more room if nothing else. The air conditioner was blasting, and combined with most people being soaking wet, everyone seemed to be freezing to death. My English class dream girl started taking her hands and rubbing them along the sides of her legs around her knees and then into her inner thighs and legs. She did this repeatedly. I watched it all from the corner of my eye. From that point on, every time I saw her hands move I turned my head and pretended that I was looking out of the window checking out the weather. The more I watched the hornier I got. It couldn't be helped really. She was so sexy and graceful. It seemed like every touch had some deeper purpose. I tried to keep my mind off of it but I couldn't. I tried to read but my dick kept moving and expanding. Finally, after a few minutes I reached a total hard on. I tried to hide it by angling my book but it didn't really work. I caught her looking at me fumbling around. Her eyes peered at my crotch and a little smile protruded on her face. She turned away and gave her attention back to the rambling professor. I thought about taking my bookbag and sitting it in my lap, but at this point, that would have pointless. I just sat there with my boner and my book for what seemed an eternity. The bell rang eventually and class was over. My hard on was still there but it had decreased a little. I threw my things into my bag and sat up out of my chair. She looked at me and smiled and said "See you next week." I said "Let's hope so" and smiled back at her. I walked behind her on the way out of the room. What a great ass she had on her. I wonder what that would look like strutting around my room in the middle of the night. I held the door open for her on the way out. She turned left and walked down the hall. I walked straight and headed out of the front door and immediately lit a cigarette. See you next Tuesday baby.

+++

I rarely dream, but for some reason I did last night. All I can remember is that you got "Fuck off" tattooed on your knuckles. You showed it to me hoping that this extreme act would finally force me to get the point you have been trying to relay to me for quite some time.

+++

What some might call alcoholism I call research. What the fuck would I write about if I didn't go out drinking all the time? I guess I'm supposed to sit here and bullshit you. I for one refuse to do that. Everything I write happened for the most part and was what I felt at the time of the typing. I couldn't make this shit up if I tried. People watching is the real fiction. The lives they live and the acts they perform are entertainment for me. I just sit back and record it.

+++

No cabs left

On the first day of a new year

Sitting in frigid temperatures

Alone and in silence

The masses have dispersed

My friends are gone

Only me and the bums

Are out this late

Monroe Drive

To Ponce De Leon

I eat barbeque Lay's chips

On the long walk

To my ghetto home

"Fucking honkey!"

They yell

Near the Church's chicken

Boulevard NE

I lower my head and keep walking

Irwin Street

Waddell Street

To Dixie Avenue NE

+++

Sundays are usually filled with mental masturbation. The TV flickers constantly as I drown myself in average movies on TBS. I find it difficult to move. I call up Bob Evans down the street and order some food. Hell, I'm just proud of myself for being able to put on pants at this point.

+++

I walk into the same bar I always do. I sit at the bar in the same seat as always. I light cigarette after cigarette until it seems like it's an extension of my own hand. A college football game blares from every TV in the place. There is the occasional clap when the team in red makes a play. I wasn't really watching the game but I stared at it anyways, I guess giving the illusion that I was really interested. The bald guy in the blue long-sleeve shirt sitting next to me tries to make chit-chat with me about the game. I just nod and say the occasional "Yea" so I don't seem too fucked up or rude to him. The seats to my right have been empty all night with just the occasional drunk walking up to order a drink.

They're out of my usual PBR in the bottle so I had to order something new. I contemplated the situation for a while but my brain was cloudy from the previous days drinking session. Finally, the bartender comes back over and asks me once again what I want to drink. I look confused and just point down at the unknown beer on the coaster near my hand. It's some German shit that I can barely read and much less pronounce. After I think my third German beer, two blonde girls sit down in the stools next to mine. I overhear them order some drink with Malibu rum in it. From the look of the drink the bartender brought them, I took it to be a rum and Coke. They laugh and whisper stories to each other and time passes slowly. I'm so bored I pretend that they occasionally are whispering about me, which I seriously doubt. I notice the blonde nearest to me is quite attractive and smokes her cigarette with a hint of elegance that only a beautiful woman can possess. Her nails are perfect and white. She had obviously gotten them done recently. I don't think she noticed me staring at them. She went to the bathroom and I glance at the other blonde. She wasn't as attractive as the other one but she was still very fuckable. In a few minutes she comes back and puts her purse down right next to me. It's very large and has a red pattern of some sort on it. I stare at it and she sees me doing it. A second later she moves the purse back into her lap. I guess she thought I was going to steal it or something. After a few minutes, she goes to the bathroom once again. While she's away the bartender comes over and talks to the other blonde. He looks at me and says "Hey Brett, do you know Samantha?" I say "She looks familiar but I don't think we've ever met." I say to the blonde "Hey how are you doing?" She nods and says nothing to me as a look of disgust encompasses her face. She wasn't very friendly, that's for sure. Her friend finally comes back from the bathroom. She sits down and they whisper some more but this time glancing in my direction. I don't know what they say but I assumed it was something about me. They finish their drinks and pay their tab and leave. They stare at me as they leave the bar. I don't know why. I take my right hand and rub my nose to see if I had a booger hanging out of my nose or something, but it didn't feel like I did. I guess some things I'll never figure out or know about women.

+++

It's not even worth writing about

Anymore

Detoxification of the mind takes longer

Than I would like to admit

The fun is over like being an adult

One small step closer to release and

Freedom

It's still poisoning my mind

Though

The yoke I carry is ten miles

Long

I run for freedom but

All I get is a bullet in the back of my head

+++

I haven't gotten laid in a long time. My mind is empty. I have nothing to write about. Writing about how my cum accidentally fell on the floor while I was jerking off just doesn't have the same zeal that fucking another human being does. I try and relive past sexual accomplishments, but my mind is still blank and the paper is still empty.

+++

Cigarettes mixed with coffee

My morning hangover poison

Booze and cigarettes my

Evening preferable poison

Frozen pizzas and two year old

Chicken fingers

Have me feeling bloated

The end result is always

The same

Hugging the toilet seat

No, not vomit spewing

Just shit

That's the real ending of the story

+++

I asked for a subscription to the porno magazine

"Big Black Ass" for Christmas

But when I awoke early on Christmas Day

It was nowhere to be found

I didn't know Santa Claus was such a fucking

Jewish cocksucker

+++

Desperation hit me

I tried to fuck the ugliest

Girl in the entire bar

My friends laughed at me as we left

But I didn't care

Fuck them

I needed pussy

Any pussy

My balls were on fire

And my brain is filled with nothing

But sex

Sex, Sex, Sex, Sex, Sex

In my head

Fucking

Cock in pussy

Wet pussy

Sucking it out of me

My balls needed release

It didn't matter from whom

That was obvious

+++

We get back to her hotel room. It was some shitty hotel that smelled of cat piss in a bad part of town. It didn't matter to me at all. I pulled down her pants and ripped off her panties. She told me to slow down and take it easy, but I just couldn't. I tried not to look at her face. It was so hideous that it turned my stomach. I tried to imagine myself fucking some gorgeous girl somewhere else in a different time. It didn't really work though. This hideous ugly naked girl in front me was my reality. I threw her on the bed and tried to put my dick in her right away. There was no foreplay and no kissing at all. I just couldn't do it. I kept trying to get it in but her pussy just wouldn't open up. I tried different positions but nothing was different. I eased a finger into her but it was still fucking dry as hell and wouldn't get wet. Of all the fucking things to happen to me! Here I am trying to fuck the most hideous women I have ever seen and I can't even do it. I sat on my knees and played with my dick. She just laid there for a minute. Finally, I had the idea that the little bottle of hotel shampoo could maybe do the job. I point at the little bottle and tell her to go and get it. She turns on a lamp and I look at her as my dick goes limp. She takes a piss and comes back and lies on the bed. She spreads her legs and pours a handful of green shampoo on and in her pussy. My dick is as limp as it could be ever be. She got on her knees and gives me a blowjob, but nothing is happening. Time keeps ticking by and nothing that she does helps. I guess I'd seen her in the light one too many times. My dick just refused to let me complete the act. I say "This just isn't meant to be" as I get off the bed and zip up my jeans. I guess I can still say I haven't fucked an ugly chick yet. Trying doesn't count, right? I walked out of the hotel room and down to the street corner where I called a cab. This was a really fucking bad idea I think to myself. The Budweiser slowly wears off as I sit on the damp street corner waiting on the Yellow Cab guy to pick me up.

+++

It's four in the morning and I nurse my beer. I take sips of yellowish beer between pumping dollar bills into a trivia machine sitting in front me. I'm so drunk I get all the questions wrong. Only drunks and low lives are left around here at these hours. A guy I don't know says hi to me and shakes my hand. I have no idea who he is. I order another beer even though I don't want it. It's my only friend on nights like these.

+++

I sit here at 12:15 a.m. in my room lit only by a computer screen. It's raining outside. It's March 7, 2006. My guts are torn up. I'm alone and I'm feeling it tonight. It would be nice to have someone to talk to right now, but there is no one. There are only empty words on a screen. I'm so alone that I rarely notice it except for nights like this where it's late and dark. I think this town is killing me a little bit at a time. I have no close friends here. I have a few that I can have a decent conversation with every once in a while but they have girlfriends or work at shitty strip clubs during these hours. I am often a solitary human being. Some people can't take it, but I can. They say that the solitary time in jail fucks with your mind. Yet, here I sit a free man in my own sort of solitary jail that I call my room. I have nowhere to go and nothing to do to pass the hours. All I can do is write, draw, or listen to music. It's a mundane existence but I deal with it.

+++

I wake up sweating. The stench of my body is overwhelming. I bring my armpit closer to my face and take in the full aroma of it. It almost makes me gag. I wipe it on my sheets and then switch it around so that the stink is now by my feet instead of my face. I pull the sheets up near my neck and try and go to sleep, but my body refuses to let me. I lay there for hours starring at the ceiling and letting the feel of urine wanting to come out of me build up. I stir, but I can't find the motivation to make it seven feet into the bathroom. I laid there for several more minutes until I just start pissing on myself for reasons that I can't explain. It's the best feeling I've had in a while for some unknown reason. A puddle of it begins to form underneath my back. The warmth of the urine calms my body as I slowly drift into deep REM.

+++

"Hey Mom can you go get me a Chick-fil-A biscuit?"

"Sure honey."

"Do you want anything else?"

"Yea, get me a Coke and some hash browns as well if you don't mind."

"Ok honey, I'll leave in a few minutes ok."

The door shuts to my room and the lock is turned. I wait patiently for my Mom to leave the apartment. I hear movement and the sounds of items being touched or moved. I hear a toilet flush and I hope that is the end of the beautifying process so I can get her out of the apartment so I can get this girl out of the apartment that's in my bed. I get on all fours and peek under the door. I hear my Mom doing the dishes now. Damn it! I wish she would hurry up so I can get this girl out of here and get some fucking sleep!

"Fuck, I wish she would hurry up!"

"Hey, Adrian are you still awake?"

"Fuck."

I pace the floor and light a cigarette. I smoke it until I taste the filter and then put it out in a blue glass sitting on my nightstand. I grab a CD case and take it into my bathroom so I have something to read while I take a shit. I wasted five minutes taking the shit, but it seemed to be an eternity on the stool. After I wiped my ass, I went back on all fours and listened for more sounds from my mother. She is still here in the apartment. I sit on the edge of my bed and watch a little TV. I finally hear the front door open and shut. I wait a few minutes and then go into the living room and then into her room and I peered out of the window. I watch as she gets into her car and shuts the door. A few seconds later, I watch as she pulls out of the parking lot.

"Goddamn it Adrian, wake up!"

"She's gone so now's your chance."

I notice she is paying me no mind and has her back turned to me and is slightly snoring. I shake her a few times and she finally wakes up.

"You gotta go now baby!"

"Ok, get me my bra."

"Where the fuck is it?"

"I don't know, you're the one who took it off."

I scour the floor for this elusive bra, which is harder to find in complete darkness than you might think. I find it in the corner of my room laying over one of my shoes. I throw the bra at her and it lands next to her on the bed

"Hurry up, the Chick-fil-A is just down the street. She will be back in no time so hurry the fuck up would you?"

"Fuck you Brett."

"I don't need this bullshit."

"Look, I don't have time to argue about this, just hurry up."

"Shut up you fucking asshole."

"You were only nice to me so you could fuck me weren't you?"

"Probably, what do you expect? I'm a scumbag and you know that."

"I know, but I was hoping you really weren't like that."

"Well who knows, just hurry up and get dressed and get out of here. We can continue this philosophical statement about my character at another time ok?"

"Get me my pants and my shirt."

"Where are they?"

"Over there by your pants, are you blind?"

I open the door to my room as she puts on her shoes and stumbles towards the front door.

"I want some water before I go."

"Ok, hold on for fuck's sake would you."

I search for water in my fridge, but I'm out

"I'm out of water baby what else do you want?"

"Just give me some tap water then."

I search for a glass and grab the yellow plastic one which was the first one I saw in the cabinet. I pour the water into the glass and hand it to her. She stands there drinking it slowly.

"Would you hurry up please, she's going to be back soon."

"Just take it with you I don't like that glass anyway."

"Here."

She hands me the glass and I throw it in the sink. I lead her towards the front door and unlock the deadbolt and then unlock and turn the bottom door handle. I push her out of the front door with me following closely behind her.

"Bye."

"Bye, I'll call you later."

I close the door behind her; mission accomplished. Maybe now I can get some fucking sleep. Women are such a headache sometimes.

+++

It's 2:43 in the morning. Where the fuck are you? You're out fucking some other scumbag aren't you, you little fucking whore! I know I rarely bathe and never have any money and I leave PBR bottles wherever I finish them, but that's no reason to leave me God-fucking-damn-it! Wait, do I even have a girl? I don't remember anymore. I don't even know who I'm yelling at. These last eight years have been a blur, everything runs together sometimes.

+++

The clock ticks

Striking sixty times

Per minute

That's my curse

The curse of too much time

It humors me to see

People complain that they don't have enough

Of it

Feel free to have

Some of mine

+++

"You fucking bitch!"

"I can't stand you."

"Why are you still here?"

"I thought I kicked you out of my life months ago."

"I should have my fucking head examined for fucking around with you."

"I love you."

"I love you too."

"I'm sorry baby, I'm just stressed out."

"Will you make me some food please? I'm fucking starving here."

"I don't feel like it."

"I'll just call and get some pizza delivered."

"I don't want any pizza."

"Don't worry I'll pay for it."

"Fuck that, I have money"

"If I wanted pizza, I would pay for it myself."

"I ate pizza yesterday anyways you lazy ass bitch."

"I want something actually cooked here."

"I feel like some lasagna."

"Please go make me some will you?"

"No, I'll just call Dominos."

"Fuck that!"

"Now get in the kitchen and make me some lasagna."

"Fuck you asshole, make the Goddamn lasagna yourself."

"Who do you think you are, Garfield or something?"

"I love you baby."

"I love you too baby."

"Come here and give me a kiss."

"Ok."

"Now how about that lasagna huh?"

+++

Food, I don't even enjoy it anymore. It's just something I do when my stomach starts churning. It should be done in solitary confinement. Watching or hearing other humans eat nauseates me. An image of large pigs slopping out of the trough fills my brain. The only company I want during a meal is a strange baritone voice blaring out of my crappy pawn shop TV.

+++

The dirty blade

Enters my arm

Then my abdomen

There was no call

No reason

No choice

But to do it

I needed to feel

To know

That I was still alive

The blood spilt on the floor

Running down my body

Onto the floor

Confirmed

That yes

I was still somewhat human

+++

Donald Rumsfeld called me a terrorist today. I'm un-American because I hate
the state and wish for more redneck American soldiers to die. They're tapping
my phone now without a warrant thanks to this right wing Christian Gestapo
regime. It doesn't really matter since no one calls me anyways. I use my mom's
bible as toilet paper these days. It's a little rough but it sure feels good as a
matter of principle. Allah strapped another bomb to my chest since I had
nothing else to do really. I'm the perfect anti social suicide bomber, just without
the unkempt beard.

+++

My greatest line from the past few days was telling a girl that her ass belonged in
the Smithsonian. Damn, I'm such the charmer.

+++

I haven't showered or shaved

In days

I don't really feel the need to

Does it really matter to look the best you can

If you never leave the house

And go out of your way to avoid people

+++

We kiss on your mom's couch as the TV flashes in a glare off of the patio window. I nervously slide off your pants and socks, but your blue bra stays on for some reason. My heart beats out of my chest as your soft hand moves its way down my pants like a slithering snake. I feel your hand grab my dick and then touch my balls. Your hand goes to unzip my pants and I let you. My hands are shaking and I hope you didn't notice. We kiss a few more times and then I get on top of you in the missionary position. I inch my dick toward your vagina. I'm about to feel what it's like for the first time. I have dreamed and obsessed about it for years and finally my chance had arrived. I grab my dick as I look in your eyes and my head touches a pussy for the very first time. I go to put it in but you hear a noise. What the fuck was that? Fuck, fuck, fuck, your mom is back home from work. I hear a key enter the door lock and then a turn. I jump off of you and grab my clothes into a little bundle and I hold them in my arms. You open the patio door and run upstairs to your room. I make it out the door and turn a sharp right. I take a peak and see your mom browsing through the mail on the kitchen counter. I fumble trying to get my clothes on and then I leap off the balcony and onto the ground. I take one last look towards your house before I turn and run through the woods in your mom's backyard.

+++

I was in Wal Mart today. I usually try and stay away from the place but sometimes it can't be helped. I happen to live in a town where there are few options to buy shit I actually need like garbage bags, toilet paper, and caulk. I was walking the endless aisles in the food department looking for a box of Chicken Helper. That's an obvious sign of being alone if you ask me, well that and the Tostino's Pizzas for one that were in my buggy of steel and wheels. I was browsing the shelves for my Chicken Helper. The first shelf contained Hamburger Helper. The second shelf contained Tuna Helper. The third and final shelf I hit the jackpot, there before my eyes was finally my elusive Chicken Helper. The third shelf was filled with ten different kinds of Chicken Helper. I'd just made it to the four cheese pasta one before I heard a voice say "Hey son." I turned to my left and there standing before me was an old man wearing a plaid shirt and a floppy hat that just said "Jesus." The hat stood out in my mind as being very cheaply made. It was probably made in Burma or something, no wait Burma is Myanmar now, whatever. The old man in a very heavy Southern accent asked to look at my tattoos. I turned towards him and held out my arms. He went on about being in Korea and how all his buddies got tattoos over there. It was truly fascinating to hear an old man ramble on about events fifty years old but I just wanted my goddamn Chicken Helper so I could get the hell out there and go home and cook. I turned my eyes back to the four cheese pasta and the old man made a gesture with his hand. His outreached wrinkled hand was holding a card. I grabbed it and didn't look at it at first. I went back to my Chicken Helper and he finally slowly walked past me. I chose the Italian shells for my kind of Chicken Helper and threw it in the buggy. I pushed on and finally looked at the card. It said "Have You Found Jesus?" and continued the whole spiel about how Jesus is the only way to redemption and heaven. I ripped the card up and threw it on the floor and pushed on towards the checkout. The only thing I want Jesus to do is end my shit before I become like that motherfucker. Old and trying to save souls in Wal Mart on a Monday afternoon is a pathetic way to die slowly if you ask me.

+++

Little black children asking me questions

I don't have the answers to

I give them chatter and propaganda

188

But never the truth

I wish they would play somewhere else

Besides the parking lot in front of my building

But they don't

They yell and they scream

And only shut the fuck up

Between the hours of eleven and seven

That's when they get the energy to scream

The next day

All day

Sometimes when I'm pulling in

I dream of running their asses over

And putting an end to them

I imagine their little legs resting underneath

My Goodyears

Their own dogs feasting on them as mid-day snacks

They bring me a liver and I throw it as far as I can

Playing catch has never been so much fun

+++

I sent a girl an e-mail today while I was sitting in a coffee shop here in Holland. It was freezing and raining so I dipped into the first café I saw. Two people were smoking something in back on a couch. They laugh and giggle every so often. The coffee warmed my hands a little but they were still shaking as I tried to type. It will be Christmas soon. I have no other means of correspondence at the moment, so the free usage of internet access was appreciated and worth the overpriced black coffee. The small Indian man asks me if I need anything else. I say "No thanks, all I need is black coffee, foreign cigarettes and Amsterdam in the winter." He laughed and walked away.

+++

I have Joy Division on tonight. Their songs depress me and I like it. Maybe I should make mix CDs filled with nothing but Joy Division by the thousands and leave them in bathroom stalls and on empty benches, that way everyone else could be bummed out as well.

+++

I was standing on the top of the hill near my shitty apartment. I sat on my skateboard as the day slowly faded away. No cars were coming my way. It was a red light so it was now or never. One big push and I was flying like a maniac down the hill. The wind pushed my face and hair back as I flew past the abandoned mill and grew closer to the new video production building on the corner. All was quiet and well and then all of a sudden "Where did that patch of gravel and sand come from?" were my thoughts as I laid face first in the pavement. Then my mind went blank. I could hear the wheels still turning on my board as I laid there in peaceful silence. All of a sudden pain shot all over me, from my knees to my head. Blood began to flow from my elbows, head and knees. I looked over and saw a guy smoking a cigarette in front of a nearby building. I drug my corpse over to the sidewalk and just sit there for a while picking the gravel out of my body. A few minutes later I walked home.

+++

My bar

It really is my bar

My numerous tabs have paid the rent more than once

The choice of stained wood chairs

Padded or unpadded, it's my choice

My luxury

The glimmer of the bar at around 3 a.m.

I know well

Very well

The oval paper coasters

But sometimes square

I just walk in and everyone knows me

And what I drink

I don't have to say a word

Just give a nod

Now that my friend is

The life

+++

I'm leaning against the bar. I'm by myself as usual. My back is to the bar so I can easily people watch. Ideas and useless information fill my head. A beautiful girl walks by me. I watch her the whole time. Every step and every motion she makes is glorious and magnificent. She glances in my direction and gives a small smile. I just look at her and all her beauty and I'm frozen with lust.

"I should go after her."

"Just do it you fucking idiot."

"What will I say?"

"It will be something stupid and idiotic."

"Who cares, just go you pussy."

I take a few baby steps in her direction. I see her sit down across from a guy in a pink collard shirt.

+++

Hey whitey, you're running out of suburbs to move into. Your security gates have failed. Your brick walls are being chipped away. Your fat lazy cops can't get all of us. We're coming more and more. The niggers, spics, and the gooks are coming for you whitey. Where are you going to run to next whitey? Where's your next suburban oasis of boredom and professionalism? I hear Idaho is open and likes whitey. But we'll be there one day too, maybe not in your lifetime but definitely in your kid's lifetimes. We might fuck your daughter one day and probably beat your son at basketball. What are you going to do then whitey? Move to Canada?

+++

I got thrown out of the Masquerade because one of the security guards saw me drinking some of my friend's beer. I snuck back in under the back chain link fence and one of the guys in the Anti-Heroes snuck me up the backstage stairs. I got one good stage dive in during their set before the previous bouncer saw me and threw me into the floor face first. I was dazed but I got up on one knee. I saw several of my teeth lying on the floor next to my leg. Blood was streaming out of my mouth. Some of my friends grabbed the dude before he could do anymore damage to me. I walked outside and sat on a small brick wall on North Avenue and smoked cigarettes for a while. I must have been quite a sight sitting there covered in blood and trash and dirt from the Masquerade floor.

+++

I had one leg on the floor and one leg propped up on the toilet. I guess I wasn't paying full attention when I was shaving the bottom of my balls and I hit a vein with my razor. Blood shot out everywhere and started covering the floor. I grabbed a white towel and wrapped it around myself. I dialed 911 with one hand and held my bloody balls in the other.

+++

I took a walk

Down the serial killer trail

Near my apartment

Massive ant-hills appeared

Around a corner

Next to a headless doll

And other trash

I sat in the brown dirt

That riddles South Carolina

And watched the ants for a while

Their symmetry was amazing

I had a new respect for ants

After this day

I rose to my feet

And I stomped on the ants

I killed them and destroyed their home

I sat back down in the brown dirt

And watched them again

+++

Kneel to your gods, to the covers of various celebrity magazines and beautiful faces flashing on the screen of MTV reality shows. Worship them, praise them, and relate to them, if you wish. Or even worse, be jealous of them and the lifestyles they live. Chit-chat over drinks about who's fucking who or whose new marriage is on the fringe of breaking up. It's all pointless and a waste of time and breath anyways. It's all gloss paper and pixel alignment. Never mind those starving niggers in the Sudan or those seven-year-old gooks in Singapore making the shoes on your feet with the little swoosh on it. If it's not screaming at you or getting in your face and hassling your normal routine, it must not exist in the world?

+++

I watch them at a distance. There are three of them in a row on my right side and maybe five or six of them on my left side. They look like little drones to me. They carry heavy bookbags on their backs; metaphorically speaking, they are carrying monkeys on their back. They limp into classrooms now but they will be limping into huge high rise office buildings soon enough and probably even for the rest of their lives. They will exist under bad lighting and will call a cubicle home, taking shit from their boss and hoping for a raise. What trivial lives they will live.

+++

I was awoken by screaming

My Mom screaming at me in fact

She grabbed me by the shoulder

And drug me downstairs and outside

There in the driveway

Was my little blue bag of porno magazines

She had found my stash

While I was out last night

I watched in horror as she covered

All my Juggs and Clubs in lighter fluid

And then lit a match

She said "Good riddance to this filth you little pervert"

What a waste

It will take me years to build it back up to par

She will not be getting a Mother's Day card from me this year

+++

Sometimes I know too much. I've come to the realization that there is absolutely no point to life. I'm constantly fucked up and bummed out about it. I've always kind of known that, but it fucks me up hardcore these days. School, work, women, is there any point in doing any of it? I don't believe in anything anymore. I'm stumbling through life without point or direction it seems. I'm working on being a better person because that's about all I can do at the moment that makes sense to me. It seems when I was younger I didn't need a point. Life was about having fun and that was it. Life was just grand hanging out with my friends and skateboarding all day. It seems simple now but I never had a care in the fucking world and it was great. Being an adult fucking sucks ass! Its basically get a job to have the money to buy shit and pay rent, over and over and over again for like fifty fucking years. If that doesn't seem like the most pointless shit in the world, I don't know what is. I suppose I'm not having fun or something anymore, that, or my idea of fun is getting old. But hey, there are only so many things a twenty-six-year-old guy can do on a Friday night. I'm in a fucking rut and I know it. It seems like I live the same day over and over again like my own personal "Groundhog Day" or something. I sleep and then I wake up and fuck around and take a shower. Then I fuck around some more and go do my shit. I get something to eat and I come home and watch TV. I dick around some more until three in the morning and then I do it all over again. I'm fucking boring now and I don't like it. I get drunk, I womanize, and I shop, but that hardly fills my time anymore and has become somewhat stagnant to me.

+++

I masturbated five times yesterday and I don't even know why I did it. Maybe it was just boredom. Dealing with women is too difficult sometimes. Some days it's just better to jerk off a bunch and be done with it. At least there's no awkward silence after I cum. I smoke a cigarette and go on about my business as if nothing had happened. Sundays usually make me do some fucking crazy shit; I will admit that. The ass end of a drunken four day binger keeps me from thinking clearly. The neighbors downstairs always wake me up at around ten in the morning on Saturdays and Sundays. I don't nap, so once I'm up, I'm up for the long haul. After the fifth time of jerking off I could hardly function. I thought I was going to pass out going for a lime flavored Gatorade that was in my refrigerator. I think the words chronic masturbator and me pretty much go hand and hand.

+++

Is there any hope for the human race?

Everyone's the same

Boring and pathetic

One can live their entire life these days

Without every having to actually critically think

We take what we're offered

And most are happy with that

But I'm not

Where did my hopes and dreams go to die?

Lying behind me in a past life

Of innocent and believable childhood dreams

Parties by the pool

Surrounded by beautiful women in bikinis

Drinking exotic beer from Europe

Well piss on them then and their perfect lives

A farce and a hoax

My life is no Budweiser commercial

Your smiles are killing me

While the grenades of muffled despair

Are a curtain call to freedom

+++

The boredom strikes on time as always. Like a clock working without the orange. I wake up the same everyday to the same doldrums and the same apartment. I go to bed to the same doldrums and the same apartment. I could change apartments but it would be the same again after a while. I could get new possessions but even they would become normal and predictable just as the ones I have now are. I could get a girlfriend or a wife, I guess. But look at the divorce rate these days. She would get old and predictable as well. I could always get a more interesting and profound job I suppose, but even that would lose its luster after a while. And really, what's the point of working anyway? Every job I ever had led to a dead end from the start. And really, was I put here on Earth as a living breathing creature to sweep some bathroom floors or cook chicken fingers for some drunken asshole in a bar? I could travel the world. But then again that takes a bunch of money the last time I heard. Maybe I need to get in touch with my primal instincts. Maybe I'm just here to eat and fuck. That seems as logical to me as paying taxes or buying a house with a white picket fence and having 2.5 kids stuck in some suburb somewhere. No wait, that sounds like some metaphor for hell now that I look back on it. I just want some answers. But they're answers unfortunately that no one really has. My guess is as good as yours. There can be no master's degrees awarded in this subject. Fuck it, now where did I leave that beer?

+++

"Hey Brett," the young beauty says.

"Yes," I answer in a mumbling tone.

"I want you inside me."

"I want you inside me now."

My heart starts racing a thousand miles an hour. Pussy is all that fills my brain. The smell of it, that unmistakable smell like no other thing on this fucking rotten planet. I tear off my clothes like they're on fire. I leave my Hanes underwear on though. The young beauty reaches over and slides my underwear down exposing my cock. She takes it into her petite mouth and begins sucking away like a Hoover vacuum. I grab the back of her hair and push her down further. She gags as I smile.

"Now I'm gonna give you what you really want."

"Fuck me; give me that fucking big cock now."

I pulled off her panties with ease and started playing with her perfect little hairless beaver. I toyed with it as I kissed her. I eased one finger in and then two, and I pushed in as deep as I could. I laid down on top off her and eased my rooster inside of her.

"Oh God yes," she whispered in my ear.

"I've wanted you for so long."

"I've been watching you from my window."

"I just love how you mow our grass every two weeks."

I started pounding away on her. I watched as her perfect pink-toned flesh moved with every buck I gave her. I started breathing heavy and I felt my balls tighten up. The cum was near, I could feel it dying for release. Just before I came, I pulled my cock out of her and just held it in my hand. She looked at me with a very confused and disoriented expression on her face. I'm sure her thoughts were "What the fuck is he doing?" I just smiled the biggest smile I could manage and I said "Do you really think I would ever let a twelve year old make me cum?" then I started putting on my clothes.

"Get fucking dressed."

"You know your Mom gets home in a few minutes."

I went into the hallway bathroom and took a big shit. And let me tell you it smelled the house up fast. My young beauty was working on her 7th grade science project as I stumbled out the door and out of her life until I come back in two weeks to mow the grass once again.

+++

In my mind everyone that shouldn't breed does, and sadly they often even have the nerve to breed more than once. The people that actually should be breeding, like myself, don't. Why, you ask? Because, I actually worry about what kind of parent I would be or even if I would want a child to grow up in an America filled with hate, war, mass consumerism, and mass ignorance. Sorry, I have common sense; I know it's rare these days. If I ever do have a kid I'm moving to fucking Europe or Africa. America is no longer a place for innocence or even compassion.

+++

Clowns of sand

The safety is off

My lighter not a gun

A pasty housewife from Akron, Ohio

Rides a horse naked

In an open field

Provolone cheese is rotting

Leeway for a dyke

Posturing for position

Coupons for pool cleaning litter my mailbox

Yet I have no pool to clean

Gonorrhea leaks from my kitchen

Faucet

While a cat shits on my

Front door

Unshaven pubic hair

John Holmes

A xylophone sits

Alone in a corner

Next to a Milli Vanilli 45 speed 7 inch

Questions posed

From a Keebler Elf

Asterisk

Cough medicine bought

But not paid for

The London Bridge

Arizona landscape

The road to my spleen

+++

The hangover of death has found me. I wake up at eight and take a piss and chug a bottle of water and an old Budweiser I find hiding in the back of the refrigerator behind some old cheese and a flat bottle of ginger ale. I try and sleep again, it doesn't work. I turn the TV on. I flip through channels but there's nothing on but old movies and talking heads on CNN. I feel my stomach churn and soon it cramps up. The need to take a shit hits me like a freight train. I make it to the toilet just in time to drop all the horrible food I ate drunk last night. It was quite the mixture of water and solids from the sound and smell of it. I rub my face and dig the crust out of my eyes. I wipe my ass and try and lay back down. This does no good. I start sweating so I get up and turn the air conditioner on and lay back down. Again, trying to sleep is futile. I get up and scratch my balls and light a cigarette. This is going to be one long fucking day.

+++

I think if there is a God he really hates you women. Besides all the vaginal problems like periods or yeast infections and childbirth and having to spend all that money on tampons and gynecologists, he screwed you in other ways. God also had a sense of humor for a lot of you in the looks department. It seems like a lot of girls out there either have a great face and the body of a ten-year-old boy, or a porn star body and the face of a Gremlin. I wonder if I was given the choice what I would choose? A great face or a great body, now that's a hard one I must say. No wonder all you bitches are getting into plastic surgery, now I get it!

+++

I think my father was right. I am a loser. Pretty amazing that he noticed this trait about me at such an early age. He's not worth a shit either, but I give him credit for that one. Come to think of it we're all losers. No one finds any answers. There's no point to anything or any of it that people determine to be so important. We're all losers in the end. We all end up buried in cheap assembly line produced coffins under headstones of last names and birth dates. That jokes on all of us. We all have that in common.

+++

I passed a lonely shoe tonight when I was riding my bike around the abandoned waterway. It was an old Nike high top with a blue swoosh on the side. I wondered who possibly lost an old shoe out in the middle of the street. How could that shoe have survived all these years and then be suddenly discarded for no apparent reason? I want to get to the bottom of this story but there are no answers, only theoretical possibilities. Yes, these are the mundane things I ponder on late night solitary bike rides here in Myrtle Beach.

+++

I cuddled with her after I came inside of her. It felt weird. After five minutes I said I had to take a piss. I lied just to get out of it.

+++

When I got home I jerked off to a porno magazine I've had for years. Amazing how they can do what you couldn't. Maybe I need to start fucking better looking women or something. The girls I take home drunk from the bar are losing their luster now. All that effort and sweat for that? I pounded away on you for hours but nothing came out. My dick shriveled up to a miniscule size after a while. I kept stroking it but it didn't respond. That's when it's time to put on my pants and get the hell out of there.

+++

Images of women

Beautiful women

Big breasted women

Women who would want

Nothing to do with a loser

Like me

They're out of my league

One look at me

And

Then

One look at them

And that would be apparent

All masturbating

With large wooden crosses

Blood flows

They wear no crowns

Not from hands

Or from their feet

But from their

Beautiful wet cunts

+++

At 7:34 a.m. I wake up from a nightmare. I rarely dream but I did tonight. I don't remember what it was about but that's usually how it works. My stomach churns. I might throw up or I might just have to take a shit. Time will tell I suppose. My pillow stinks of dried sweat so I turn it over. I lay there and stare at the ceiling. I find the remote on the nightstand and turn on the TV, but nothing's on. My stomach churns even more. I can feel my body eating away at my fat reserves. Drive-thru breakfast at Chick-fil-A pops into my head at 8:32 a.m. I find my pants in the corner where I left them last night. I wear no shirt, only a Minor Threat sweatshirt that I find in the closet. At 8:45 I was out the door and greeted to overcast skies and freezing temperatures.

+++

I was walking down Euclid Avenue today. I kicked a beer can that was against the curb. I noticed that it hardly moved so I bent down to check it out. It was a full twenty-four ounce can of Miller Genuine Draft. I wiped off the top of the can with my white Black Flag shirt and cracked it open. I never felt cooler in my entire life. That was my first beer, hot from the Georgia sun and thirteen years old.

+++

My cock moves in and out

Slithering like a snake inside of you

Testicles tighten

Ridiculous expression on my face

My bottle of white out has been released

My seed runs down your thigh

And onto my sheets

Forming a stain

That I will sleep in

For the next eight hours

+++

I got a letter today from this really cheesy lawyer that has his own cheaply made commercials that run on local television a lot around here. Old Harry Pavilack is after me to collect a debt I owe to some credit card company in Atlanta. I actually feel great about it. If anyone was gonna sue me I'd rather it be old Harry Pavilack than anyone else. He's still not getting shit from me though. I'm poor Harry, so shove it up your bald Jew ass!

+++

I resent this time of year with all these holidays seemingly never ending. Let's see, there's Thanksgiving, Christmas, and New Years all right on top of each other. All three have ceased being even remotely important to me over the years. I just want to tune it all out and be left alone. This is pretty hard to accomplish though. You pretty much have to avoid all social contact as well as all television, radio, and internet connections. In four days, I must go be around these strangers that are supposedly my family. I don't know them, nor do I want to. Frankly, I know the Indian guy at the gas station I frequent to buy cigarettes and newspapers better than them. But yet, every year I take that five hour journey to see these strangers and hear their screaming kids and the summing up of the previous years' actions into several simple generic sentences. All I can do is bring a few good books so I can tune in and drop out.

+++

Her walk of shame

Many women have faced it

Wherever I have lived

Sun blinding your eyes

Hair tangled

Clothes wrinkled and unkempt

Debris from my floor clinging

For dear life

My cum still inside of you

Running for the ground

+++

Every bar I go to I see one of you there. It never fails. Past memories and failures fill my intoxicated brain. We both know what I did to you, to all of you. Cum, fucking, naked on your bed and every position, I remember it all my darlings. It's like remembering the scenes from a bad movie on TBS late at night. It's there resonating in my head and playing over and over on multiple screens. I stumble to the bar and order another drink, vodka please my dear with the huge tits. I try not to look her in the eyes anymore than I can. It's an uncomfortable position to be in, I can tell you that. It's like going back to the scene of a past crime, under screaming bright lights in a house of Gestapo. I pound my drink as fast I can and get the fuck out of there.

+++

Jealousy's evil twin headed snake

Headless horsemen teaching me on a blackboard

Raw chicken consumed to live dangerously

Dead batteries fueling my hate

Eyes peering from

And thoughts of madness take over

I see what I shouldn't

Suicide by butter knife is what the paper said

What a tragedy

He had so much talent

What a waste

The strike of a match to relight past desires

Covered in a puddle of piss

Free to think but shunned for saying

Dummy hat in a corner

Alone and somehow happy

Masturbating near the window

Life and all its glory

Cum stained paper

Flushed away

Nothing but a memory now

As are you

A forged new path must be undertaken

The dimly lit hallways of my mind

Are my only guides

+++

Sorry kids, but I hate to break this news to you. Santa Claus is a Jewish fag from north of the border. I saw Jesus giving him a rim job the other night while all the little reindeers looked on and cheered as Santa gave Jesus a reach around. If you don't believe me, just check YouTube in several days for photographic evidence. It will be right next to those tapes of other fictitious characters and events like Bigfoot and the Holocaust.

+++

I met this girl in a sleazy bar recently. Her name I can't remember, but who cares anyway? It was late, that's all I know. I stumbled in drunk as usual and managed to mumble the words "PBR." I sat by myself in the corner; which is my usual spot. I sit there alone most times. I like it, no humans bother me in that spot. I often overhear conversations of theirs and that's enough to know I would never want to meet them. There I was contemplating life and shit, and the next thing I know she's there next to me talking my fucking ear off. I mumble a few words between her pauses. I call her a "Dirty bitch" and she still sits there. After a while of this odd foreplay, we leave the bar and head to her place. As soon as the front door is open, I'm all over her, groping and kissing her and pulling her clothes off. I kicked her cat out of the way and it hissed at me, little shithead! We stumbled into the bedroom and pulled her panties off. I licked her for a few minutes. Then I said "This is going to be a night you will never forget, I won't remember you, but you will fucking remember the name Brett Stout for the rest of your life." I pulled out my cock which was as hard as I have ever seen it. I grabbed some hand lotion that she had by the nightstand and rubbed a gob of it on my cock. I told her to lie on her side. Before she even knew what hit her I shoved my dick right in her tight little ass. She screamed in agony. She told me to stop, but I just started to pound away as hard as I could. I told her it would be over in a minute and to just be open minded and experience new things since she was such a brilliant person. I fucked so hard I was about to pass out. As I came the sun was rising and blinded me for a second. My dick popped out of her tight little ass like a jack in the box. I sat there and looked at her for a few minutes. My only thoughts were "You're a whore." I lit a cigarette and wiped my cock off on her pillow. I left her laying there with a strange look on her face. I grabbed her pack of cigarettes and a Coke out of the refrigerator on the way out. The damn cat was in my way again so I kicked it really hard this time. I slammed the door and stumbled out of her apartment trying to figure out how the fuck I was going to get home this time.

+++

Her pussy lips look like

A butterfly's wings

It tastes good

Hell, it even smells good

I lick her clit

After fumbling around

Trying to find it for twenty minutes

I nibble and suck on it

She squirms and

Digs her red nails

Into her couch

A few minutes later

She squirts clear cum

On my face

I grab a pillow from

Her couch

And wipe my face on it

The cum is still on there

Though

Along with a bunch of

Cat hair

Goddamn it!

+++

I was browsing on Amazon.com today for some new books to read. I was writing on a Post-it note with a green pen I had gotten from the bank a while ago. I started thinking about how much I hated my bank. They're always trying to screw me in some sort of way with lame ass fees and charges for every fucking thing I do. I pulled my pants down and stuck the pen halfway up my ass. I moved it in and out a few times, for good measure. I pulled the green pen from the bank out of my ass. It had a little bit of shit on it, and yes, it smelled like shit. I went into the kitchen and got a Ziploc bag from underneath the sink and I put the pen in it. The next time I head down there to the bank I'm gonna sign my check with it, and then hand it to the teller.

+++

I kissed her again at the beach today. We stood near my car. There was an old lady sitting in a white Cadillac to my right. I didn't mind if she watched. I got sand on my lip as I was kissing her. I backed away and wiped my lips off with my old Ramone's shirt with the hole in the upper right corner. I then proceeded to kiss her again. After we made out for a few minutes, she said goodbye to me. I had a boner as I got into my car.

+++

I split my pants today. They're my favorite pants to be lazy and hang around the house in. They're ratty blue plaid pants my Grandmother gave me years ago for Christmas. Goddamn they're comfortable as shit. The hole keeps getting bigger with every movement I make. It's right by my crotch. I think one of my balls was hanging out today as I went out to get the mail. Who cares though? Ed McMahon says I'm a millionaire motherfucker!

+++

At 9:56 we were watching Blue Velvet

On your small TV set

By 10:13 you scratched my back

At 10:23 your annoying dog had to take a shit

At 10:25 you were outside walking the dog

So it could take a shit in the neighbor's lawn

At 10:27 I paused Blue Velvet

By 10:28 I finally found my lighter

At 10:30 I smoked a cigarette on your porch

By 10:34 we were kissing on your uncomfortable couch

With animal hair all over it

At 10:42 I put my right index finger in your wet pussy

At 10:47 I had my face buried there

By 11:13 my jaw hurt

At 11:15 you were sucking my cock

By 11:27 you had cum on your large fake tits

At 11:28 I got you a towel

+++

We wake up and fuck again. I came inside of you once again. My bed has been soiled and smells of sex. I smoke a cigarette as you get dressed.

"Go to Popeye's and get me some fucking chicken!"

You say "Ok."

"I want an eight pack of chicken fingers, mashed potatoes, and a sweet tea."

You say "Ok."

"I don't have any money; can you get it this time?"

You say "Ok."

"I spent it all last night getting us drunk."

She leaves and I turn on the TV and wait. There's nothing much on but I watch Rambo II on TBS while I wait. It sucks not having cable, goddamn it!

"It took you forever."

"I'm sorry I got lost."

"You're a fucking moron!"

"You've lived in this town your whole life, how do not know where Popeye's chicken is?"

"I'm sorry."

"Fuck your sorry, I'm fucking starving here pancake."

"Why are you calling me pancake?"

"That's the nickname I gave you."

"Why."

"Because, every time I fuck you it's like fucking a goddamn pancake."

"You just lay there like a deer in headlights while I pound away."

"That's mean, I'm fucking leaving" she says.

"Fine, get the fuck out of here pancake."

"And never fucking come back you stupid bitch!"

I threw my chicken dinner at her as she left. It hit the door instead of her. I continued to harass that bitch from my kitchen window until she got in her blue compact sedan and left. I picked the chicken off the floor and ate it on the futon alone and in silence.

Zombie Pills

I only had a couple of beers last night. I wanted to be straight for the beginning of this trip. I took a cold shower, not by my choice. Ghetto apartments like these rarely have hot water. I finished packing the rest of my shit up and was ready to go. I grabbed a sandwich at Blimpie and I finished eating just as my friend John got home from work.

We got rear ended by some white guy on Moreland Avenue on the way to the bank, but no car wreck could stop me this day. We checked the damage to both the cars. It wasn't really that bad on either vehicle. We said that we were in a rush and had to go. A man with a dumbfounded look on his face was our view as we sped off from the scene. I got to the airport about an hour early. The line for international flights was so fucking long. I had to stand in line next to some Irish guy who smelled like mothballs for an hour. I don't know if he had been hibernating in some attic for several years or what the deal was. I tried to stay far enough away from him that I didn't have to smell him, but that was pretty much impossible.

I offered the lady behind me to go ahead of me in line, but she smartly declined, bitch. I breezed through security and customs. My only hassle was the fact that I had to take off my shoes. All I needed was a flower and some patchouli and I could have been a fucking hippie. I hit the gates with a half hour to spare. I took a quick precautionary shit and chain-smoked as many Marlboros as I could before I got on the plane. I could hardly contain my excitement. I felt like a little kid again. My journey that was months in the making was finally here. So long America, welcome to the unknown.

I lucked out and got an aisle seat. It would have really fucking sucked to get stuck in the middle seat; an eight hour flight being stuck in that seat would have been torture I can't imagine. Like a rat in a cage I guess, being poked and prodded. I grabbed Henry Miller's "The Air Conditioned Nightmare" and my Queens of the Stone Age CD and zoned out. My reading was interrupted when the stewardess cracked me in the leg with her stupid fucking cart. Beef or chicken was the choice for dinner. I chose beef, which looked like some kind of tenth grader's science experiment. But, it was edible. The in-flight movie was to be some movie with Will Smith, no thanks.

No one can really sleep in an airplane, it's impossible unless you down a bottle of sleeping pills and a bottle of vodka. I couldn't tell if I was asleep, awake, or dreaming. The next thing I know the landing gear is going down. I was in Amsterdam at last. It was the next day here because of the six hour time difference. I hadn't moved in seven hours, my whole body was a cramp. I got off the plane at 7:30 a.m. I felt like the living dead. It was either culture shock or insanity. Everything was in Dutch; I had no idea where I was going, so I tried to stay close to the other people on the plane. I had my first cigarette in days or hours, who knows at this point. And I must say, it was one of the best damn cigarettes I've ever had. This one was even better than the one after you get laid.

I exchanged my hundred Dollars for seventy Euros. The money here is really cool, with lots of different sizes and colors. Though, there are way too many different kinds of change here. I counted ten different ones and some of them weigh at least a pound. The shit weighed my pants down so I threw them in my bag, probably never to be seen again. I tried to figure out what train I was supposed to be on to get to Amsterdam. I asked a few people which was the right train, but no one spoke English. I was getting pretty pissed off by now so I just got on the next train I saw. The train said to Central Station, which was where I needed to go. I stood on the train so I could see out of the windows. Culture shock hit me like a ton of bricks; everything in this place was so different. After about thirty minutes I made out the words Central Station on the intercom and got off there. I was hauling my heavy ass luggage around looking stupid when I noticed a sign that said Central Station Den Haag. Obviously, I had fucked up somewhere along the way. I wandered around for a while trying to figure out how to get back. I finally figured out that the train that I was just on was going all the way back to Amsterdam. I had thirty minutes to waste. I bought an orange Fanta soda that came in a bottle that looked like some sort of sculpture disaster. I got my first real peek of Holland. There were bicycles everywhere I looked.

It was so cold and damp out. The people watching was incredible here. The women that I saw were so natural looking. No make up and boob jobs for them. I wasted the thirty minutes smoking Marlboros and freezing to death with my orange soda, and it was the most serene thirty minutes of my life.

I lugged my baggage back on the train and we headed out. I can already tell that hauling this heavy luggage around is going to be a real pain in the ass! I struck up a conversation with a young guy sitting across from me on the train. I saw him reading an English newspaper so I figured what the hell. His name was Marcus and he was from Den Haag and went to school in Amsterdam. We shot the shit for a while and he said he would help me find my way to Amsterdam, which I did appreciate. He was a real cool guy. He said he wants to go to New York really bad. I told him he wasn't missing very much. But I guess if I lived in Europe and heard what a great place it was, I would want to go to. Go observe how fucked up we are, and then get the fuck out.

We finally made it back to Amsterdam. He showed me the way out of the train station and pointed to where I could catch a cab. I gave him a stern handshake and thanked him for his help. I waved goodbye and made my way over to the cab stand. I asked the first guy I saw to take me to the Hotel De Gerstekorrel. I threw my bags in the trunk and we were on our way. How cool, every cab in sight was a fucking Mercedes. This place keeps getting weirder and weirder. A five minute ride later and we were in front of the hotel. The lady at the front desk said I couldn't check in for an hour. I left my luggage there and said that I would be back. The first bar I saw was across the street so I headed over there. It was ten in the morning; I was in a foreign country, so why not have a beer? I ordered a drink called Duvel and chugged it down. I was the only guy in the bar so I started talking to the bartender Tony. He was from England,

and a damn nice guy as well. It wasn't until three beers later that I noticed that Duvel had nine percent alcohol content. It was no wonder why I was already feeling drunk. I thought I'd just turned into a big pussy or something. I'd already started slurring so it was time to go. I told Tony that I was going to take a nap and I would be back to get drunk again later. I grabbed a couple of slices of pizza on the way back and I finally checked into my room. It was time for a nap.

I slept until six. I was still wearing the same clothes from yesterday, I mean today. Who knows now what day it is? I felt rejuvenated, but still a little fucked up. Whether that was from the booze or the jet lag, I don't know? I went back across the street as promised. Tony had left, so I ended up meeting the new bartenders. They were all really cool as well. I bullshitted with them for a few hours, but I was dying to go and see the red light district for myself. It was a pretty amazing sight for the first time. There's a beautiful canal running through all the sex and drugs. The pimps and drug dealers harassed me the whole time I was walking around. All I heard was "Hey blondie" from every side street I passed. I said "No thank you" to the first couple of guys that asked me to buy their fucking X or Coke or whatever. That eventually got old, so I just stared at the ground and didn't say anything. It was weird walking by seemingly normal looking storefronts and seeing nothing but huge dildos and porno magazines staring back at me. Man, what liberal people these Dutch are.

The girls in the windows surrounded by red lights were all incredibly beautiful. I couldn't believe it. I didn't see one ugly girl. If they weren't prostitutes, they would probably turn me down if I asked them out on a date. I stopped for a beer at a bar called the Old Sailor Pub. The bartender didn't speak English so I just pointed at something on tap and he gave it to me. There wasn't much going on there so I headed down the street to another bar called Excalibur. The placed looked like a real dump from the outside, so I figured I would fit right in. Motorhead was playing on the jukebox when I walked in, and there were motorcycles and swords hanging all over the walls. I started out drinking Grolsch, which tasted like shit, so I had my first Budweiser in Europe. The label was a little different; it just said "Bud" in big letters. I ended up meeting this couple from of all places Ohio. The guy was so drunk that he bought me a few drinks just because I was from the States. Eventually, he went to the bathroom, and his wife slid over and sat next to me. The first words out of her mouth were "Do you want to have sex with me." I just sat there shocked. I was like, what about your husband? All she said was that he wasn't a fag but that he liked to watch her fuck other guys. She told me that he paid a Swiss porn star a thousand dollars to fuck her several nights ago. I shot the shit with her for a while, she was a wacko, but she was interesting I will say that. I said "No thanks" to the sex offer though, if she wouldn't have been so ugly and fat, maybe. She tried getting a few other guys to go home with her, but none did. I guess they got bummed out and left eventually. I was pretty fucking loaded when I left the bar.

I wondered around for a time, the bright red lights flashing the word "Sex" were even more interesting than before. Girls were knocking on their windows and yelling at me to get me to come in. I felt like Dante for a minute there. I guess I was more entertaining than their usual clientele of bald married men; that, or maybe I just looked like an idiot tourist, who knows? There was this one girl I couldn't stop looking at though. I passed by her window like six times. She was such a beautiful creature; my thoughts were only of how could she be a whore?

On my way out of the red light district I saw my basement whore again. I just stood there and looked at her. It wasn't long before she opened her little door and asked me if I wanted to come in. I hesitated and made lame excuses why I couldn't, but I stood no chance and went inside. She closed her curtain while I lighted a smoke. The room was empty. There was only a bed and a couch and an ashtray. We talked for a minute about the usual bullshit you talk to someone about just before you're about to have sex with. She said that she was from Italy and here for three weeks in Amsterdam making some money and then she was going back. I wanted to ask more, but she said that my time was ticking away. I gave her the price of fifty Euros for a "Suck and fuck" as she called it. By the time I got my clothes off and on the bed I only had like ten minutes left. She gave me a blowjob with the condom on, which I didn't really feel. I had a semi-hard on which was good enough I guess so I stuck it in her. I pumped away for a few minutes, it was nothing sexy here, just mechanical. Soon, she said that my time was up. I hadn't cum yet, so I tried giving her like twenty Euros to let me finish. She said that it would be fifty again to finish. I only had twenty so I put my shit on and left. I stumbled back to the hotel from there, past the drug dealers and the pimps once again. "X, Coke, X, Coke" was all that I heard on the way back to the hotel. The pizza stand was still open when I got back, two more slices please! Back to the room to jerk off and eat pizza, what a day!

Seattle Piss State Free

I drove from Vancouver to Seattle today. It was a lot easier crossing the border this time than it was before, although I still got hassled a little bit. I had to wait in line for about an hour before I got to the actual border. These guys on carts were selling ice-cream to border crossers every ten feet, it's got to suck being a Canadian ice-cream salesman. You would think they would sell something a little more useful like a Cuban cigar store on wheels or something. Hey tourists, smut and duty free whores are right this way. I got asked the typical questions by the border pigs, why was I in Canada and what did I do while I was there. Then the pig asked if he could look through my van, I knew they were going to look anyway, so I said yes. He said that my t-shirts looked new and that I didn't declare anything. He asked if I was trying to sneak t-shirts across the border. I said that I've had these shirts for years and my secret to keeping them new looking was that I never washed them. I knew a smart ass comment would get me pulled over, and it did. The pig told me to park and to go and see the customs people inside. These pigs think it's their god-given right to be fucking assholes and get away with it. I went inside and they took my driver's license and I had to fill out a bunch of forms. I waited while the pigs searched my van. They said I was good to go, and soon I was back in the good old USA.

If the streets weren't so filthy, I would've kissed the ground. What was my first stop in America, a fucking Taco Bell in Binghamton. There was a cute girl working the register and I talked to her while I waited on my tacos. I finished eating my three dollar combo meal and I headed back down the road. My next stop was Seattle. I got pretty lost when I got to Seattle; I was trying to find 2nd Avenue which is where the backpacker hostel was. The place looked like a dump, nothing but a bunch of heroin-addict looking assholes hanging out in front of the place. I decided to scratch that idea; I wasn't looking forward to staying there anyway. What is it about the Pacific Northwest; everyone looks like a fucking junkie. I guess because the sun never comes out everyone decides to drink coffee and shoot smack. I pulled the van over and I busted out the budget travel guide. I found this hotel near the University of Washington called the College Inn. It ended up being a cool little place, and it was about as no-frills as a hotel can get. For my thirty dollar a night hotel, I got no television, air conditioning, and only one shared bathroom on each floor. Room number 209 looks as small as a bunk on a fucking submarine. Luckily, for me, it's kind of a cool day in July so not having any air conditioning won't be a big deal.

I decided to check out the town so I headed up University Avenue. I went to three great record stores up there, and I found some really cool CDs for a dirt cheap prices. After going to all the record stores I grabbed a couple slices of pizza and I walked around for awhile. I decided to go and check out this seedy little bar called Earls. The bartender was a big ass German lady, I would hate to have sex with her, I could imagine her being pretty stern. I ordered a Budweiser and I grabbed myself a barstool. There were a lot of women in the bar, a few of them were checking me out but not talking to me, which is usually the case with women and me. A bunch of drunken people came in from a wedding reception and they were loud and really annoying to say the least. They kind of ruined the cool vibe of the place as soon as they came in. I was talking to the guy sitting next to me at the bar and he said there was a good dive bar up the street that I should check out, and so I decided to get the fuck out of there and go and find it.

Once again, I had gotten bad directions and I ended up wandering aimlessly around town. I saw this little bar as I was walking and I decided to go in. The bartender was a punk rocker and he told me the dive bar was three blocks over. The dive bar was called the Monkey Bar and after I finished my beer I headed over there. It was a cool place and I met a lot of cool people. The only negative thing to the place was that the band playing really sucked. I don't remember their name but I do remember their bass player was hot. She was wearing this little red wife-beater and she didn't have a bra on, so you could see her nipples for days. I was going to go and talk to her, that was, until she started kissing all over some other dude. It was just what I needed, a rocker girl with big nipples, oh well some day soon maybe. I talked to some guys about my trip, they seemed pretty interested in my stories from the road. Last call in Seattle is 1:00 a.m. which is pretty fucking lame, so before too long they kicked everyone out of the bar.

I was drunk once again walking towards an unfamiliar hotel, and once again I got lost somewhere along the way. I finally found a gas station; I say if I'm going to be lost I'm going to do it with a big grab bag of Doritos. I felt like I was just aimlessly wondering around Seattle. Along the way I really had to take a piss. I saw a dark alley, so I went over to take a piss. About halfway between my leak I saw blue lights go on. It was one of those situations, do I try and zip up or do I finish pissing? I'm the type of guy who finishes. The way I figured was, if he took me to jail, at least I'll go with an empty bladder.

He walked up to me and he asked me for my driver's license. He then asked if I knew that urinating in public was a crime in Washington. I said that I was lost and I had to take a piss, and what was I supposed to do? He ran my license and asked me some questions. He said that I had pissed on a church; I got punk rock points without even knowing it. We ended up talking for awhile; the cop was actually kind of cool to me. He said not to do it again, and he said that I could go. He even gave me directions back to the hotel before he left, thanks a lot Seattle Police Department. I was totally on the wrong side of town, I was fucked once again. I finally made it back to the hotel where I beat off, ate my chips, and went to bed in no particular order.

Doing Time at the Free Clinic

My appointment at the free clinic wasn't until 3:30 this afternoon. The building was over on 21st avenue in a non-descript yellow brick building. I arrived about fifteen minutes early and smoked cigarettes like a man on death row and sweated my ass off in my car until it was time to head into the clinic. I walked up three small stairs and peeked inside as I took the last few puffs on my cigarette. It was now or never I told myself. This is what must be done for peace for mind and also to save a ton of money, especially since I couldn't afford to actually pay for this test otherwise. I walked in through the swinging iron doors which creaked and croaked as I pushed them open. Several black men turned their heads and looked at me for a brief second and then turned away.

There was a small thin wall separating two different front desks. I really wasn't sure which one I needed to go to, so I picked the one on the right and walked up to the unattractive overweight white lady at the desk. I said "Hi, I'm supposed to have an appointment at 3:30." She briefly looked me and then went back to typing on her computer. There's something about working for the government that seems to just make people overly miserable.

She asked me my name and all of the usual personal information these types of government places always want to know like my social security number and my phone number. I told the truth to most of the questions that she asked me. She handed me a slip that I also had to fill out. "Yes I'm white, no I don't have any money, I only have twenty-seven bucks to my name and yes I'm a college student." I checked all the appropriate boxes and handed it back to her. She said "Take a seat and we'll call you soon."

The cramped waiting room under bad white neon lighting was pretty much filled up. I stood for a few minutes against a wall, and then when my feet started going to sleep I found a seat near the window and sat down next to an old black man. The room smelled quite bad, like overdue baby diapers and death. I browsed the crowd and felt a lot better about myself. Everyone in the waiting room was black or Mexican. There was only one other white person besides me, which was a pretty good looking woman with three fucking loud ass kids beside her playing with some sort of plastic cars and trucks.

I got the feeling most people in here were waiting on someone. There were no magazines of any kind and the only reading material were a few pamphlets on pre-natal care. I just sat there and tried not to think about where I was or what I was about to do. After about five minutes the white woman with all the kids was called into a room on the right. I was relieved to get rid of those annoying screaming kids. I figured out after a little while that all the people with kids went to the door on the right and pretty much everyone else went to the door on the left. Both sides should come with a sign reading "Poor trash of society this way" with an arrow pointing just in case some were illiterate. I laid me head against the white brick walls and tried to close my eyes, but this was almost an impossible place to relax at all.

"Stout, Brett Stout" came from a voice in the corner. I got up and walked towards the door on the left hand side and proceeded in. A huge white guy around 6'4 and 250 pounds wearing a white doctor's coat led me into a small room down the hall. He said "This is Denise and she's gonna take a blood sample from you. Come into this room and see me after you're done" as he pointed to a door on the right two doors down from the one I was heading into.

I sat in the chair next to Denise. She was really hot the more I looked at her. We chit-chatted for a few minutes while she got the needle ready, she said "Well, which arm do you want it in?" I said "I guess it really doesn't matter." I pointed to my right arm eventually and she put a large rubber band just above my elbow. The veins in my arm started puffing out of my skin. She rubbed a little alcohol pack on it then stuck the needle in me. She drained a decent sized syringe worth of blood from me and put the cap back on the needle. She said I could hang out for a second and then to go and see the doctor down the hall. I said ok and thanked her for sticking me, and I don't really know why I did that. I should have been cursing her instead.

I waited a few minutes in the non-descript white walled room and then headed down the hallway. The doctor's door was partly open. I poked my head in and said "Hi." He told me to come in and sit down. The room was very small with just a desk and a few things placed neatly on two sets of shelves. He said "I need to ask you a few personal questions. Don't be afraid to be honest, I've heard it all before." I said alright. His first question was how many people had I slept with in the past six months. I said "Oh, two or three," since I couldn't really remember the actual number.

That seemed like a decent number to not be a total whore, but not to be totally pathetic either. He wrote down my answers as I blurted them out. The last question was "Do I always use condoms?" I was honest and said "I try most of the time, but hey, sometimes I get drunk and just wanna fuck doc." He chuckled a little and finished writing. He said "Well, are you ready?" I said "Yea I guess I'm as ready as I'm ever going to be."

My heart started beating as we entered the examination room. I stood there with my hands in my pockets as he got his gloves and what seemed to be a large foot long Q-Tip from one of the drawers in the room. He put the latex gloves on and said "Alright, drop your pants." I took a deep breath and tried not to think about the fact that I was about to have a strange guy grabbing my dick and putting a large Q-Tip inside of it.

He said "This is going to sting for a second." He then grabbed my shriveled up penis and rammed the Q-Tip all the way inside of it. My whole body reacted and the ten second sting was almost unbearable. He didn't just poke it inside of the head, he swirled it around as well which made it even worse. He finally pulled out the large white Q-Tip and placed it in a small specimen bag. I pulled up my pants as he did this and tried to regain my composure.

He asked me if it was that bad. I said "Well, I wouldn't wanna get it done everyday but it was tolerable, you motherfucker!" I didn't really say that last part, but I did think it. He handed me a card and told me to call back in ten days. He did say that if he found anything really bad he would give me a call. But if he didn't call, I should assume that everything was alright as far as the AIDS and STDs were concerned. He said "Here, take some condoms with you, and please try to wear them all the time from now on." I said "Sure, I'll do what I can Doc."

I grabbed the card and the large bag of condoms from his hand and thanked him. I gently walked past all of the losers in the waiting room and through the front iron doors and finally I was back to reality as I walked towards my car. I took a sip of hot sweet tea I had and lit a cigarette. Fucking great, this is going to be the longest ten days of my life.

I Fucked your Mother, and I Can Prove It

Things picked up for me last night. I met a few friends at a bar here in town around 9 p.m. My older lady friend from Detroit called me back around 11 p.m. She's in town and wanted to hang out, which basically means o have sex. I hung out until around midnight and then I sold my friends out for a piece of ass. I would expect and hope the same from them. I made it to the bar she was hanging out at just in time for last call. I ordered a Budweiser in the bottle that she paid for and drank it slowly. I got half of it down before I dumped it in the trash.

My older lady friend from Detroit rode with me to her place. She kissed me before we pulled out of the parking lot, and I won't lie, I got a pretty fucking hard boner. It's hard enough to drive drunk as it is, but it's even harder when you have a girl with her hand on your cock. She always stays way up in North Myrtle Beach, which is a pain in the ass drive from where I live. Luck was on my side once again, and I made it there without going to jail.

We tried to go into the bar next door but we missed last call by half an hour. I recommended that we just go have sex in her room and she agreed. We ran into one of her friends who was making out with a very ugly fellow in the hallway of her rented condo. I got stuck hanging out with him while the girls went to the bathroom. He tried the boring chit-chat routine, but I really didn't care.

I just wanted and needed to breed, and anything that didn't involve that didn't hold my interest. I found a large bottle of Jagermeister and sugar free Red Bull in the fridge. I made myself a couple of shots and chugged them down while they were in the bathroom doing who-knows-what. My older lady friend from Michigan finally came back from the bathroom after what felt like thirty minutes. Every bed in the house was taken except for a little tiny bed in one of the side rooms.

Her friend was already sleeping in the other bed in the room so I suggested that we just go out on the beach and fuck. After walking over to the beach, and past several more random nasty people making out on some stairs, we chickened out of doing it. She was complaining about getting sand in her ass or something like that. I just wanted and needed to fuck plain and simple and I didn't really care where it went down. I suggested my car, but she wasn't going for that either.

We went back up to the room to get more booze. We opened the front door and saw her friend having sex on the pull-out couch with the guy I was talking to earlier. Thank God I couldn't really see them, but I could definitely hear their voices. I wonder what all these married women are like back at home in the suburbs of Detroit. I'm thinking they're probably not as interesting or insane as they are here. When they come down here, their hotel room turns into a drunken sex orgy that Caligula himself would be proud of.

I somehow got talked into having sex on the midget bed while her fat friend was sleeping not six feet away from us. I ran my hand up her thighs and played with her snatch until I felt my hand covered in juices. I ripped off her pants with the panties still inside of them and pulled my dick out and mounted her as soon as I could get on top of her. I pounded her for what seemed like ages. We were pretty loud, so I knew the whole place knew we were having sex. I was covered in sweat and felt like I was running some kind of ten mile road race.

After a while, her pussy was getting a little dry so I asked if she had any lube. She said there was a little bottle of KY in the nightstand that was next to the bed. I scrambled through all kinds of brushes and bras before finally finding it. I lubed my cock up and stuck it back in. I got a glimpse of the clock. It read 3:30 in the morning; I had already fucked her for almost an hour. She kept saying how she loved me inside of her and how she wished she could fuck me all the time. Little does she know that if we did it all the time it would probably be more boring than the sex she gets from her husband.

But really, people say all kinds of stupid weird shit while fucking so it was no big deal. Whenever I have sex with her, I think of her at home with her kids, making them peanut butter and jelly sandwiches and telling them to go take a "Time out" in their room when they piss her off or doing something bad. I feel sorry for them really; it's a good thing they have no idea what I do to their mom when she's on vacation! It would probably give them an eating disorder or something if they ever did find out.

We fucked in just about every position that was possible for two really drunk people. I lasted a long time after I lubed my dick up with KY. I made her start saying all this nasty shit about fucking her tight little pussy and I eventually shot my load of cum all inside of her. We were both exhausted and we were both dripping with sweat. My cum started coming out of her pussy and was dripping all over the sheets.

The bed was too fucking small for two people to sleep in, so I made up some lame excuse and got out of there. I had sex and that's all I wanted. I hit Highway 17 at around 4:30 in the morning. It was a long boring drive home. Iggy pop kept me company on the drive home. I didn't run into any cops on the way home, thank fucking God. It wasn't too long before I was passed out in my own stain free full sized bed.